CHAMPIONS OF PLEASURE

CHAMPIONS OF PLEASURE

'May I ask a favour?'

'Of course.' A short nap had refreshed Goemon considerably and he was idly surveying the pale, naked beauty of his hostess.

'You are of course my guest, and it is unmannerly to impose but ... I have four apprentices. They are good for little but helping me prepare myself, fetch things, and so on. Soon, however, there will be customers asking after them. And though some men pay well for virgins, I do not purvey women for sleeping with. There are houses for that. So if men are going to sleep with them after one of my entertainments, they must be accomplished in what they do. To preserve *my* reputation, you understand.' She bowed slightly to him. 'Could you perhaps take their virginities for me? I realise it is a bother, but it's so much better than doing it mechanically.'

Goemon nodded, speechless. 'How many did you say there were?' he finally managed to ask.

'Only four.'

'Bring them on,' he said weakly ...

CHAMPIONS OF PLEASURE

Anonymous

NEXUS
A Nexus Book
published by
the Paperback Division of
W.H. Allen & Co Plc

A Nexus Book
Published in 1989
by the Paperback Division of
W.H. Allen & Co. Plc
Sekforde House, 175-9 St John Street
London EC1V 4LL

Copyright © Akhige Namban 1986

Printed and bound in Great Britain by
Cox & Wyman Ltd, Reading

ISBN 0 352 32427 9

Chapter 1

A bright spring sun shone warmly on the myriad islands of the Japans, more peaceful now during the reign of the Tokugawa clan than they had been for two centuries. The government of the Tokugawa shoguns, ruling in the emperor's name, was new and still untried; like the morning sun, it was still on its way to the zenith. Flat, straight-edged paddy fields lay verdant with the first plantings. Bound by the fields lay the houses and palaces of Edo, home of the shogun, ruler of the land in all but name. More than four hundred miles away, in a bowl of mountains that sheltered Miyako, home of the emperor, All under Heaven in nothing but name, two people sat amid a lush spring garden, enjoying the pleasures of the season.

A fish plopped in the still pond, disturbing a floating willow leaf. A pebble beach led up from the water to a small thatched structure. The hut consisted of little more than a covered wooden-floored verandah and a small open room centred on a hearth. On the hearth reposed a kettle, hissing and bubbling over a small charcoal fire. Tea implements were racked nearby, ready for use.

The man on the verandah wore a tall black gauze hat, loose robes and trousers, and an erection. He fanned his rouged face languidly. The woman's head rested on his thighs. She nibbled delicately at the erect prick before her, moistening her mouth occasionally from a red-lacquered sake cup. The strong liquor burned pleasantly as she applied it to the quivering erection. Tremors occasionally shook the man's frame, though they were not reflected in his face.

She moved her lips slowly up and down the erect brown shaft. Slowly she approached the plum-shaped head again, sucking in the almost tight skin. A tiny clear drop formed at the tip of the instrument, and she licked it up with a slow movement of her tongue tip. She opened her mouth and changed her position so that her head over-looked the manroot. Her many layers of brocade robes rustled as she moved. Tied loosely, they fell open, revealing a plump pair of white breasts. She lowered her head as if letting go of a great weight, and the prick filled the warm cavern of her mouth, reaching to her throat. Her lips clamped, and she raised her head again. The man's breathing quick-ened imperceptibly. She lowered her head again, allowing her teeth to scrape, not too painfully, against the erect velvety rod. Then she hollowed her mouth and pumped at his organ. His hand dropped to her long, glossy black hair, and his fan stilled. There was still no expression on his face.

There was a crunch of gravel from the side of the

pavilion. Someone approached wearing heavy wooden clogs. The woman gave two quick sucks and was rewarded with spurts of thick, creamy come that filled her mouth and ran down her throat. She rose to a kneeling position, adjusting her robes and covering her white tits, while a voice called from outside.

'Mizuno-no-Kami, are you there?'

The man in the pavilion looked at the woman with him and indicated his prick, the glow now starting to fade and droop, its surface still glistening. She shook her head, and reluctantly, he covered himself up. Very unsatisfactory, he thought. He hated being interrupted.

'Yes,' he called in a cultured voice.

A young man came into view. He was dressed much as the other was, though his loose overrobe was covered with pictures of flowers, rather than phoenixes as was Mizuno's.

'Welcome, Fujiwara-no-Kami. Will you join us for tea? We are considering Golden Carp.'

Fujiwara bowed low. 'I was not aware that the lady Gojo-no-Satsuki-hime was visiting. I would be delighted.' He left his shoes at the entrance, beside those of the other two, and mounted to the mat-floored room.

They sat around the fire while Mizuno proceeded through the long and intricate ritual of pouring tea for each of them. When it had been drunk and praised, its utensils cleaned and admired, and a short poem composed on the pleasure of the occasion, Fujiwara noted casually that he had received from Kinki, on the coast, a shipment of seaweed 'of exquisite richness.' Mizuno bowed his thanks for the invitation. Their eyes met for a moment in

9

mutual understanding as the three made their goodbyes, Lady Gojo-no-Satsuki not forgetting to make a return appointment with Mizuno.

Sitting quietly, knees tucked under her, Oko listened to the frenzied sounds from behind the sliding door. Her heart hammered in her breast as the cries reached a peak. Her hands, which appeared to be resting in her lap, pushed against her soft mound. She rubbed her thighs imperceptibly together. The tip of her tongue peeped out between her red lips. She could feel the moisture oozing down the crease between her legs. She contemplated the peonies painted on the sliding door not a foot from her face and shivered. A lock of midnight-black hair fell across her immobile face.

A blonde girl lay on the other side of the sliding door. She was gasping, and the sweat ran down her glistening white skin. Her legs were raised vertically in the air, held almost immobile by strong hands. Her full breasts were flattened on her chest, and the pink nipples stood erect over them, glistening with saliva. Her ass was held off the mat by the power of the man, who dug his fingers into her thighs. His brown-bronze skin contrasted with hers. He was squatting above her, his weight bending her back into a curve.

The muscles of his strong buttocks drove him powerfully against her. He withdrew a bit. A long, dark cock, shining with moisture, emerged from her golden-fringed cunt. He rammed forward again as her fingers clawed at his ass, forcing him on.

No longer able to wait, he let go of her legs, and dropped his entire weight onto her. Her ass hit the rumpled mattress, and his body came down on hers with a liquid smack. He grunted as their flesh stuck together. Less restrained, she bared her teeth and bit his shoulder with a yowl like an injured cat. He wriggled as loads of sticky come rushed into her hot waiting passage. Gradually the motions subsided.

They lay there for a while peacefully. He tried to roll off her, but she held him in place imperiously. He raised himself lightly to look at her. Her name was Rosamund. Formally, at least, she was his prisoner, imprisoned by law, because she was a foreigner. Blue eyes looked back into his own. Rosamund smiled, remembering that she had once thought of being a nun. Now she was something else. In all but title, senior wife to the governor of the imperial city of Miyako, in the fabulous land of the Japanese. He was the only man who could fully please her. His shaven pate shone with sweat. His oiled topknot, usually a black brushstroke against his head, was now awry. She ran a clawed hand down his arm.

'You are getting flabby, Goemon. You need more exercise.'

He grunted doubtfully. His mistress was full of surprises, and although they were all delightful, they had a tendency to be painful as well. Rosamund knew that she could goad him with pain to the pitch of lust and aggression that she had learned to crave. He leaned forward and deliberately bit at the pink areola of a perfect white breast. She appeared to take no notice; her hand travelled down his arm, leaving four parallel white lines. He sucked and bit, forcing more of the breast into his mouth, almost gagging as the soft flesh pushed at his tongue.

'Oko!' he heard Rosamund call. He swivelled his eyes to his right. The fusuma doors slid open,

11

and his lover's favourite maid bowed low to the couple before her. Oko rose with a graceful gesture. He admired her posture out of the corner of his eye. She had not changed much since she had come into his service. At Rosamund's gestured directions, the serving girl poured two cups of tea.

Rosamund watched her graceful movements for a moment. As Oko picked up one cup with both her hands, ready to serve her master, Rosamund stopped her. She moved behind the girl and stroked her smooth hair. She squatted behind the slimmer figure and twitched off the loose robe she wore. Rosamund ran her tongue over the servant's smooth shoulder, from neck to joint, then repeated the motion on the other side. Oko did not move, and the teacup she held barely quivered.

Rosamund slipped the robe off the girl, stripping her to her waist. She hugged the slighter figure to her. Oko was conscious of the two full, soft mounds digging into her back. She was also conscious of her lord's eyes as her mistress fondled her own tiny breasts. The dark nipples rose erect against the pale fingers that teased and pinched them.

'Lay down the cup.'

Oko did as she was told.

'Come here!' Rosamund's eyes were glittering in excitement, and Matsudaira Konosuke, governor of Miyako, found it expedient to obey her. He stood before the girl, his bedewed prick only half-erect. Rosamund grasped his prick firmly and guided it into the depths of Oko's mouth.

He felt the growing length of his prick, guided by Rosamund, disappear into the warm cavern of Oko's mouth. She gagged a little, but took the entire length in. He felt the warmth of her tongue as it urgently tickled the length of his meaty shaft, while her face betrayed no emotion. Her tiny teeth scraped the underside of his shaft, bringing a pleasant pain. Still holding him in her fist, Rosamund moved him rapidly back and forth, like some giant animated doll. His erection strengthened, and the turgid tip of his cock scraped against the girl's palate. He felt the pressure grow in his balls. His hips jerked spasmodically, and he closed his eyes to savour the sensation as the first of his come spurted up his stiff channel, to dribble into her mouth. Suddenly the pleasure turned to pain as Rosamund viciously closed her fist on his tool. He almost screamed in pain as his balls contracted in frustration.

Rosamund ducked his swinging slap and pulled him down forcefully to a position behind Oko. She forced the girl forward until her golden buttocks rose to the ceiling. She aimed his prick into the valley between the girl's perfect buttocks. She rubbed the tip of the furiously purple cock along the brown valley. When he thought he was going to explode, she placed the tip into the cooling opening of the girl's lower lips.

'Now! Ram her!' she commanded, and moved his prick at the rhythm she wanted. He set to work furiously. His hips slammed against the upraised hillocks, smacking the hollow of his thighs and belly against Oko. Rosamund stood over him, her legs spread. She grasped his chin and forced his mouth against her musky bush. Golden hair covered the lower half of his face. He opened his mouth to savour the smell of her cunt, and his tongue licked out, teasing the lips, barely touching the prominent clitoris.

She twisted his head by his topknot. 'Harder! I want it harder.' This time he set to work in earnest. His hips rammed at the supine body beneath him, and his mouth dug into the willing cavern before his face. She clamped her thighs around him every time he tried to withdraw, barely giving him the opportunity to breathe. If he slacked, she would jerk his head painfully by his topknot.

At last, in desperation, he began to give her what she wanted. His teeth, lips, and tongue serviced her hungry lower mouth with abandon. She moaned with pleasure every time his teeth scraped her clit. He bit and licked harder, and her body clung to his mouth hungrily. At last the pressure in his balls was too powerful to ignore. He grasped Oko's flat breasts with both hands, and a stream of milky fluid spattered her battered interior. Her face, turned towards him, did not react, but the clipping of her cuntal channel told of the climax that took her.

At the same time, Rosamund, far less restrained, screamed in delight as his face was flooded with her salty interior liquids.

Rosamund released his head and rolled his limp, exhausted body off her maid with her foot. He lay there, panting heavily as she sat down, her glorious nakedness a complete contrast to his own sweaty heaving.

'I think I'll have some tea now.' She accepted a cup gracefully from Oko and sipped while her hand idly played with his flaccid cock.

Delicately, as a master artist should, he added a thin gold line to the painting he was working on. It was done in the old style and depicted four foxes in court robes playing at football. The tall black sugarloaf hat

14

of one of the foxes was tipping into his eye, and the artist was adding a glint of gold to the fox's chinstrap. It was a shame his paintings were so ephemeral. Soon, however, his real masterpiece would come to light. He thought of it for a moment as he worked steadily. The parts of the plan were perfect. The merchant had acquired what he needed most, and the kuge had put his own plans in motion. Soon they would all begin to move. He imagined the faint scent of blood, the clash of arms, the sound of conchs blowing victory. His hand trembled slightly, and the line jerked minutely.

'Stupid!' He slapped the girl's face in petulant anger. He did not like waiting. He would have to move soon. She tried to repress a sob. He smeared the paint over her breast, and the detailed scene vanished in smears of colour over her smooth flat breasts. Only the football remained, now a paint-stained nipple. He clenched his hand on the soft mound and drew her to him while loosening his robe.

In an old mansion in the city of Miyako, a man sat in a small room, reading a note over and over. The mansion was a rambling affair of rooms and corridors, all worn and somewhat decrepit. It was situated in a large, unkempt garden in the kuge quarter of the city – the quarter of the imperial courtier. The room was lit by a wan candle and the glow of a brazier.

The red glow of coals heating water for tea and the flicker of the light highlighted Mizuno's small aquiline nose, arched plucked brows, and smooth cheekbones.

The letter was a single sheet of white paper,

15

unmarred by the red stamp of a personal seal. Nothing indicated the writer's identity. It contained a line from a well-known poem entitled 'Before the Iris Comes,' and it was tied by a black cord intricately knotted.

Mizuno sucked in his breath. 'So, it is about to start,' he muttered to himself. 'Soon the All under Heaven will rule again, and I shall guide him in the path of righteousness. These Tokugawa scum will be swept away.'

As he thought, he sucked on his wooden sceptre, a flat piece of wood, highly polished, about a foot long. The rounded top was badly abraded from his habit of chewing while thinking. The merchant in Osaka had not yet reported full success, but apparently he was reaching his goal. Once he had secured the necessary goods, the plan would be put into action. Mizuno gazed contemplatively into the coals. He did not care for Osaka, a common, trade-oriented city, but his visit there had been useful. Soon the merchant would bring his merchandise to Miyako as instructed, and the work would begin.

He had been a soldier and was now a merchant. Impassive, he watched the masked plot unfold before him on the wooden stage. The stage was bare, decorated only by a single pine tree in a pot. By now he was used to the bare conventions of the stage, but the high-pitched singing and rigid movements meant little to him. The language was almost incomprehensible, unless you were a devotee of the No theatre. Only one thing truly drew his attention. He was fascinated by the masks: the lined face of the old man, the horned, tormented devil, the sharp-nosed fox, the fierce warrior, and above all, the mask of the woman. All were carved with exquisite skill and realism. Cool, smooth, pale, serene, it dominated his thoughts. The reality, he knew, was often different, but the smooth calmness of the mask, of the idea behind the mask, drove him forward in more ways than one

The incomprehensible plot finally came to an end. His host, who had played a part in the play, finally reappeared, dressed properly in expensive silks.

'I hope you enjoyed my poor entertainment?' the host asked.

The merchant bowed and uttered conventional words of thanks. They chatted desultorily for several more minutes; then his host suggested a stroll through the garden. Small stone lanterns lit the walks and the small pond. They stopped occasionally, for the host to point out the views. At length they reached a small tea pavilion. The host bowed the merchant to a seat.

'I have something that will perhaps interest you.' He reached behind them to a cupboard set in the wall. There was a series of clicks as of locks opening, then a grunt as the host pushed a heavy box forward. Beside it he placed a second one, longer and flatter. He opened the long, flat one first. A long, slick metal object emerged. The merchant examined it as his host held it, stroking it lightly.

'I enjoyed trying it,' said the host. 'We could use many more, and I gather you have some for sale . . .' He fumbled with the smaller box and threw the lid back. 'We have many more of these and are willing to exchange,' he said casually, watching the merchant through narrowed eyelids.

The merchant sucked in air through his teeth. The small box was full of oval gold coins, in packs of ten, each wrapped with a narrow band of paper. With two hands, the host picked up one pack and placed it on the mat by his guest.

'An earnest of our intentions. We will pay much also for powder and shot.'

The merchant looked out at the gloom. 'I shall not expect only gold. There are other things as well – land, for instance. I shall expect land – and honours.'

'Of course,' bowed the host. 'Of course.' His expression was unreadable.

'I can ready the shipment within a few weeks.'

'There is no hurry. It must be delivered to us at the proper time; all will be arranged. You will deliver it for us to Miyako,' he added casually.

'Miyako? You know I cannot enter the place. No, it is too dangerous.'

'Not at all. It will be easier for you than for us. I will be accompanying you, so any risk will fall on me as well. Miyako it must be.'

Slowly, still unwilling, the merchant nodded, but his eyes were drawn again and again to the glittering chest of gold.

Without a further word the host returned the chests to their hiding place. He then conducted the merchant to the room that had been prepared for his guest for the night. Bowing effusively, he parted from the merchant at the door to the room.

The merchant entered the dimly lit room, and a smile gradually split his face. A young woman, heavily made up, was lying on the bed. She wore a light robe dyed with pink and yellow blossoms. It was tied in front by a large bow in her soft sash. The merchant contemplated her lazy posture for a moment, then hurriedly divested himself of his clothing. A long, thick member jutted out from the

18

juncture of his thighs. Seeming to scent the girl, it quivered as a dog does.

He reached for the girl and pulled open the knot of her sash, then opened her robe. She smiled at him through red-painted lips. He ran his tongue over his lips, then spread her legs with both hands. Without pause he laid himself between the spread thighs. He searched for a second, guiding his prick with a large hand; then, finding the waiting entrance, he launched himself forward.

The girl winced as he penetrated her and drove up the voluptuous channel. His rump started a rough up-and-down motion as he pumped at her. His hands squeezed her flattened breasts, pinching dark nipples for a moment; then he slid his palms down her body and grasped her buttocks painfully. She whimpered a little at the pull of his powerful, calloused palms, but the professional smile stayed on her lips.

The rate of his pumping increased. He began grunting like a bull. Then, without a pause, he ground his hips into her, burying his pole as deep into her cunt as he could. Gobs of sperm burst from his inflamed balls and inundated her insides. Again he battered at her, then again, until the spasms died down gradually into mere jerkings of his powerful ass muscles. At last he lay on her, sunk in pleasure.

After a few minutes' rest, during which she shifted uncomfortably but did not try to remove his bulk, he began pumping at her again with as much vigour as before.

Behind him a small panel in the moulding of the wall near the ceiling clicked shut almost silently.

'Like all of his kind, he has no refinement. Only the cheapest kind of whore is good for that sort. Honours and land he wants? Well, we shall see.'

Chapter 2

It was a fine morning for a walk. Many of Miyako's residents thought the same. Pretty girls wearing gaily dyed light summer yukata and even brighter sashes were admired by young and not so young men in more sombre attire. The hills around the city wore a bright green, patched here and there by the white and pink of flowers and blossoms.

A small group of four climbed the wooded slopes behind the magnificent Golden Pavilion. First walked a giant samurai. In the manner of a masterless samurai – a ronin – his head was unshaven, but his hair was brushed smoothly and tied back in the manner of a professional such as a teacher or a doctor. Beside him walked a slighter man. His head was hidden by a bright kerchief, and his clothes and the herbal bag he carried indicated his status as a drug peddler and itinerant doctor. His face was delicately featured, but for the strong lines of determination that marked it. Behind them walked two women, one dressed in bright striped kimono. Her clothes, like her hairdo, indicated a samurai woman of means, but her springy walk and the tan of her beautiful, high-cheekboned face indicated a person who spent considerable time out of doors. Her walk was more of a stride than the delicate, mincing walk of a deferential samurai woman. Beside her walked a Buddhist nun in black robes. Her head was covered by a large hat that hid most of her features. Beneath her cowl, which she used to hide her features modestly from passersby, as was only proper, a perceptive observer would have noted a pair of startlingly blue round eyes and the smooth, white-faced features of a foreigner.

'Jiro,' called the nun, 'please cut me a spray of blossoms.'

They were passing under the branch of an old, wild cherry, its boughs a mass of flowers. The giant reached out a hand and snapped off a branch. He bowed to the nun and handed her the spray of pale pink blossoms. She smiled out of full red lips, and her hand lingered on his as she accepted the offering. The other woman laughed.

'You've done so long without her, I think we had better find somewhere to stop...' Her glance measured the samurai's length and then looked behind him at the doctor.

'Goemon,' she said, 'you are the only native among us. Isn't there an inn or abandoned shrine somewhere around here? I could use some sustenance.' She wiggled her hips, causing the doctor to lick his suddenly dry lips. The big man laughed deeply, and his hand slid down the nun's wide sleeve to her armpit. He felt the heavy, warm, sweaty breast that hung there.

'Yes, let's. I'm in a hurry, you see. There are some friends I haven't embraced in a while.' He jiggled the available breast suggestively.

'Perhaps there's a bamboo grove.'

'With a pool of water,' Okiku added, laughing. Goemon had to laugh in turn. That had been the venue of his first encounter with Okiku. 'Want to fight me again?' he asked playfully, then added, 'Come on – there's a small shrine higher up the mountain.'

The shrine was a small wooden structure with a moss-covered thatch roof. A sliding door, the wood cracked and grey, barred entry. They clapped and bowed their heads in respect before entering. The inside was dusty. A shelf on the far side held several small stone statuettes, their features indistinct from age and wear. Some cups and plates, the remainders of offerings, littered the shelf. Jiro chuckled and pointed. Behind one of the statues was a cluster of wooden phalluses of various sizes.

'The perfect place!' he cried. 'Dosojin, the cross-roads kami, will be delighted with us.' He turned to Rosamund with antipication. She evaded his grasp and headed for the shelf.

'Come on, Okiku. Let's each take one. These lazy men can't be half as good.' She selected the longest and thickest wooden phallus, longer and thicker than her arm.

Okiku giggled. 'You'll get splinters up your pussy. Besides, the men are so much warmer.'

Jiro took a long stride, and his hands dug deep into Rosamund's haunches. She sighed and relaxed back against his broad chest. 'Maybe later. When this nice horse is too tired to run. I might *like* splinters there. I like so many things there . . .'

She turned in Jiro's arms and in two swift movements dropped her robes. Her perfect leg wound around the back of his calf, and she pushed at his chest. Not trying to keep his balance, he fell back onto the floor with a crash, dragging her with him. She tore open his robe and ran nails down the length of his massive bronzed chest, leaving red weals behind.

Knowing what she wanted, Jiro simply let her undress him her own way while he entertained himself. Over his chest hung two full, red-tipped white mounds, tempting him to reach and fondle. He squeezed one of the full breasts, and she smiled down at him. His erect cock was squeezed between the two plump lips of her delicious, golden-haloed cunt. She slid herself up and down suggestively. He grinned, raised his head, and bit at one nipple, while squeezing hard on the other pendulous breast.

She leaned back against the pressure, and a cool mountain breeze played with her long blonde tresses. He jerked his hips suggestively, but apparently she was not ready. She rocked herself back and forth on the length of his hard rod, slickening the length of its underside.

Impatient, Jiro's hand slid to her hips, and he tried to raise her and free the tip of his waiting member. She resisted, driving her nails into the skin of his chest, leaning forward and biting his neck and then his nipples, and rubbing the fullness of her breasts against his sensitive nipples. At last she relented and allowed him to raise her to the level she wanted. But she still had one more trick to play. Holding her hips with both hands, Jiro searched for the entrance. She lowered a hand to the tip of the shaft to help him in, and he licked his lips in anticipation. Suddenly she slapped the tumescent member twice. The pain irritated and exasperated Jiro. He pulled her roughly to him and sank his shaft to the feather in her willing flesh.

Pleased by his roughness, she struck again, this time at his chest, thighs, and belly. Her flat-handed slaps stung his skin, irritating him still further. Without concern for her, intent only on releasing the tension and mixed aggression in him, he did her bidding. He pulled her hips roughly to him and arched his back, jerking his ass off the floor. His prick penetrated deep into her. In a sudden movement he forced her onto her back and rolled onto her, without losing the connection of their sex. Her legs were spread wide, and her beautiful rounded ass ground into the rough, dusty wooden floor.

Jiro brought his whole weight to bear on her cupping loins. Her breasts squashed under the movements of his broad chest. She squealed once in surprise, then started to fight back grimly. Her nails raked his shoulders. Her legs waved to and fro, drumming indiscriminately on the floor and on his ass as she sought for purchase. As he came down, she heaved her smooth hips at him, bucking him off her.

Using his greater weight and strength, Jiro held her down. He pinioned her hands with his own and spread his knees as far as they would go, forcing her legs into an awkward obtuse angle that lessened her ability to buck. Through all this his massive pillar continued to move into Rosamund at an ever-increasing pace. Slowly but surely both approached their climaxes. Rosamund started shuddering as she felt the crisis approaching, and Jiro's breath hissed between his clenched teeth.

Okiku and Goemon, who had been enjoying a slow, languorous fuck nearby, reached their climaxes in silence. Goemon discharged into Okiku's hungry nether mouth while tonguing a dark nipple. Still erect, he moved out of her and began running his sticky cock up the length of her body towards her mouth. Silently, using her eyes only, she indicated the other couple's coming peak. They lay back together to enjoy the show. Okiku's legs were spread, and his hand dipped into the warm, sopping moss between her legs, while she stroked his erect prick against her smooth side.

Rosamund, never one to restrain herself, screamed loudly as she climaxed. As if at a signal, the door and the boarded window of the shrine burst open. One of the three men who leaped into the room stabbed his short sword down at Goemon's exposed back. The other two, stupefied for a moment by the glorious sight of Okiku and Rosamund, were a trifle slower.

Goemon seemed to leap sideways into the air as a well-aimed sidewise kick by Jiro gave him impetus to avoid the blow. The sword stuck into the floor between Jiro's legs. The samurai twisted, still on his back, and his arching kick slammed against the assailant's face. There was a cracking sound of breaking bone, and the attacker's jaw hung loose. Jiro leaped to his feet.

As swiftly as a snake, Okiku had rolled closer to one of the attackers. His feet were bowled out from under him as she reached her staff. There was a click, and the tip of the staff leaped off and fell to the floor with a clatter. A hand's length of gleaming steel was revealed for a moment before she lunged forward and buried it in the third man's kidney, withdrew it with a twist, and buried it once more. The man keeled over without a sound, dead.

Goemon and the man Okiku had tripped tangled together. Goemon clutched at the man's sword hand, but he broke free and dived for his sword. The doctor lashed out with a kick that connected to the attacker's side. Spying his sash, he whipped it around the swordsman's arm and neck, binding the arm to the head. They fell together, Goemon locking his opponent's arm and shoulder to the floor. There were a hiss and a thud, accompanied by a scream. A weighted chain wielded by Rosamund, frantic at the attack against her man, crunched against the ruffian's temple.

Jiro found he had plenty of time. Without reaching for his long sword, as always within reach, he stood up. His two hard fists came up together. One stuck deep into the wounded attacker's solar plexus; the other drove into the soft crunchiness of the man's throat. The attacker flew backwards and fell outside the small shrine, dead before he landed.

Hurriedly the four friends started dressing. As Jiro adjusted his sash, his wary eye on the openings torn in the building, they heard a cough.

'Forgive me for bothering you.' A cultured voice, with a hint of command, interrupted their dressing. Swords hissed from sheaths, and Rosamund gathered her weighted chain. A figure darkened the entrance. It was that of a middle-aged man. His face was lined, and he wore an old-fashioned topknot that stuck up into a brush behind his head. He was dressed in plain but good dark travelling clothes. Two swords were stuck into his sash.

The man looked first at the three bodies, two

inside, one outside the small shrine building. Then he looked piercingly at the two couples before him, as if committing them to memory.

'Jiro!' Goemon's eyes slid to Rosamund, to Jiro, to the stranger. Jiro let out his breath. They would have to kill this man. Rosamund's presence was forbidden. She was officially a prisoner of the governor of Miyako, and her presence outside the walls of his mansion could get them all into trouble.

'Wait!' the stranger said in a voice of command. Then, in a quieter tone, he added, 'let me introduce myself. Hattori Hanzo, at your service.'

'Hanzo has been dead for several years!' Goemon bit out. Hanzo was a legend. He was Tokugawa Ieyasu, the first shogun's spymaster and assassin for many years. He could not possibly be this young.

'My father has indeed departed,' the man smiled. 'I have inherited.' As with many professions, inheriting a position meant inheriting a name as well. Actors followed the custom, as did master craftsmen, traders, and apparently, Okiku added mentally, assassins.

Hanzo withdrew a long envelope from his breast. 'I have a commission for you.' He held the envelope forward, facing the four, then opened it and withdrew a sheet of paper. One word was written on it in black ink, the writing firm and bold. 'Obey!' The word was partly obscured by a large red seal. Goemon, who recognised the seal, knelt immediately. The others rapidly followed suit.

'The Presence would like you to attend him in Edo immediately,' Hanzo said in an official-sounding voice.

'All of us?' asked Goemon.

'Miura Jiro, a masterless samurai and teacher in

27

Miyako, and a doctor, one Goemon of no known abode, who also bears another name, are to attend at the audience chamber in the Tiger's Gate in Edo.'

'It will be done,' said Goemon formally. In a less formal tone he added doubtfully, 'Is it known there may be ... problems?'

'All is taken care of,' said Hanzo. 'A message is on its way ordering the governor of Miyako into seclusion for ritual reasons – omens are inauspicious.'

Goemon bowed in relief and admiration. Hanzo bowed briefly to them, and the shogun's spymaster was gone.

The candle flames in the hot, stuffy room were hidden by expensive paper lampions, which also served to soften the light they shed. The lights made the rush mats glow like molten gold. The walls of the room were obscured. In the silence and the gloom, the only sound was that of breathing. The lampions illuminated the eyes of a young man who seemed to be staring at nothing. His breathing was harsh but even, and as he breathed, the nostrils of his high-bridged nose pinched together. From one corner of the dark room, a corner not lit by the lanterns, one could hear a quicker series of breaths. From the naked figure of the girl face down on the floor came a series of harsh gasps as she tried to fight the pull of the silk ropes that pulled her arms in opposite directions.

The man let out a sigh, and his eyes were drawn, as if involuntarily, to the figure before him. He leisurely took in the sight. The girl's figure was stocky, with plump buttocks that were firm in the light. Her back was smooth, but marred by stripes as

28

of old beatings, though these were peculiarly regular. Her head was shaven, something the man seemed to find particularly exciting, since his gaze lingered there longest.

He took a deep breath. 'So, a nun. I've not had one such, if you discount the girls who serve mountain priests. But they are nothing more than common whores. It will be interesting.'

'Who are you?' gasped the tied girl. Her neck twisted in a futile effort to examine her surroundings. She tried to raise herself but only succeeded in bunching the muscles in her buttocks and back. 'Let me go. Please let me go. I'm not very good. I – I'll not tell on you.'

'Open her legs,' the man commanded in a soft voice.

The bound girl quickly crossed her ankles in mute protest. Two figures bounded at her from the corner in which they had awaited their lord's orders. They were two young girls, twins, their faces, hairdos, and clothes all alike. Each one fastened onto one ankle, and they pulled in opposite directions. The girl on the floor struggled and cried. She twisted and managed to release one foot, and promptly kicked one of the twins in her face. The opposite twin promptly bit her ankle. The bound nun yelped, and the man smiled thinly as the other twin reestablished her grip on the errant foot. A faint trickle of blood ran down the powdered chin.

Both twins threw themselves backward, and the legs parted until the girl was stretched painfully between her two grinning tormentors. Hurriedly the two girls loosened their sashes, and each attached her sash to an ankle. Keeping the sashes taut, they tied them to the room's corner posts.

Special brackets had been sunk into the wooden pillars for their lord's amusements.

'Is she a virgin?' he demanded sharply.

'I'm a virgin. Please, I'm a virgin. Don't have me. I've never had a man, and I mustn't. The prioress will be so displeased. She'll send me away'

The girl's last words ended in a wail. One of the twins had crawled forward rapidly. Her rich gown was open, shadows hinting of the naked figure within. She stuck her finger into the shadowy crack between the prone girl's thighs. The finger penetrated easily despite the dryness of the hole she encountered. The twin looked up and grinned. 'No, lord. She has been penetrated. She's lying. She's no virgin.'

Casually the man stretched forth a hand. He stroked the shaven pate lightly, and the bristles scratched against his hard palm. The hand descended lower, tracing the curve of the jaw, then seized on the point of the chin. Quick as a striking snake, the fan held in his other hand slashed at the bound girl's cheeks.

'Don't lie to me! You have had a man. Tell me about it!'

'No, no!' she moaned. 'Never a man. No!'

He looked at the twins, perched near the rising buttocks before him. 'Put your claws into those hills,' he ordered.

Ten long fingernails dug into the smooth brown hillocks before them. Spots of blood appeared, and the man licked his lips. The naked girl writhed on the floor screaming.

'Tell me!' he repeated. 'Tell me about your first man!'

'No man! No man!' gasped the prisoner.

'How, then?' he demanded. His voice was a dead flat as before. Only his eyes seemed excited at the sight of blood.

'I'm a novice in a nunnery. The – the prioress ... the other nuns ...' She stopped, and her head fell forward onto the floor.

'So, you've been loving with other women? But that would not affect your maidenhood.' He struck again, and she screamed. 'Tell me, in detail, how you lost it!'

'I was playing ...' started the girl in a choked voice. 'I was playing with myself. I was teasing the lips ... the lips down *there* ... with my finger ...' Her voice grew stronger as she was caught up in the memory.

'The feeling was so good. I licked my finger and smelled my own smell on it. There was a faint trace of the prioress's taste too. She had welcomed me and then, in the evening, welcomed me again in her room. She has a beautiful body. I love her. She rubbed me all over, then herself all over me. And I came. I'd never come before. That was the first time. Then she showed me how to rub her body, particularly the lips and the little nubbin.

'I was doing that when one of the two girls who serve her came in. I tried to cover myself, but she made me stop. She pushed me back and started kissing my nipples. The other one came in, the one who looks so much like her. She started kissing my other mouth. It lasted for a long time. We changed positions. I felt lips and fingers and breasts on me down there. Then there was a wave of pleasure that was so intense I thought I couldn't stand it. A mouth was between my legs, another was sucking at my thighs, and two warm, heavenly, dewy bushes were beside my head, and I was licking them alternately.

My body jerked, and wave after wave rolled over me. Just as I came, one of the twins shoved her finger into me. There was a momentary pain, and then it was forgotten in the delight I felt.'

She stopped her recital. While she talked, the twins' hands had been lightly pinching her buttocks. Now their fingers stole insinuatingly down the crack of her ass. One finger lingered teasingly on the clenched hole between the mounds of her buttocks. The other twin's finger continued downward, through a rapidly moistening forest of crisp straight hairs, and scratched impatiently at the entrance to her channel.

'Twins?' said the man sharply. His palms lifted the shaven head so that he could look directly into the eyes of the girl before him.

'I... I don't know, lord. They look so similar. Maybe they are cousins. I was there only a few days before your men caught me...'

The man smiled in the dark. 'Twins... twins, you say. It will be interesting. Yes, very.' He looked as if blind at the faces of the two twins whose hands were busily digging into the girl before him. She started to writhe and moan, whether from the pain of her bent neck or from the pleasure of those probing fingers, it was hard to tell.

Holding on to her chin with one hand again, the man loosened his robe. His prick, hidden till now, sprang erect.

'This is my sword,' he snarled suddenly. 'Study it. With it I punish and reward.' He giggled suddenly. 'I've only got one, but it will have to do for two.'

She regarded the instrument with fearful fascination. It stuck up proudly from a thicket of black curls. The shaft was thick and dark. A head the size

32

of a large plum faced her, and the hole in its tip, oozing a colourless liquid, seemed to weep at her in sympathy.

'Lick it!' he commanded. Sharp pinpricks in her cunt and asshole from the twins' fingernails emphasised the urgency of obedience. Her small, soft, pink tongue emerged hesitantly, and she tentatively licked the warm, slightly moist shaft. She repeated the motion, and the monster seemed to grow and sway before her eyes. With his free hand he took hold of the shaft and pressed the knob against her cheek, then her eyes, her forehead, the rest of her face.

His motions became more frenzied. 'Don't stop licking!' he commanded. Whenever the rod or its head was within reach, she complied.

'You're not licking!' he snarled. He beat the head of his prick frenziedly against her face, using it as a club to bruise and hurt. She whimpered fearfully. The blows of the fleshy bludgeon were not particularly painful, but the man was twisting and bending her neck almost to the breaking point.

Suddenly he seemed seized by a fit. He rammed her face up against his belly. His prick mashed against the length of her face, 'Lick it! Lick it!' he called in a strangled voice. Through a mouth twisted by the pressure, she barely managed to extrude the tip of her tongue and touch the shaft. It vibrated and jerked at the touch. A squirt of something wet and sticky splattered against her cheek and closed eyelid. It was followed by a gush of the stuff as the prick throbbed and spat against her face.

He let go of her suddenly, and her head hit the tatami mat with a thump. She was crying silently.

'Come here and clean us!' she heard him order.

The twins scampered up to her face. Two heads bent forward side by side. One of them lapped at her face, licking up every trace of the sticky come. The other twin deftly scooped the drooping male member into her mouth. Red lips moved its length, collecting every drop of sperm. Cheek to cheek, the twins smiled knowingly at one another. Above their heads they could hear their master groan, 'Ugliness – I *hate* ugliness and dirt! Clean it properly...'

He was breathing heavily again, the tied girl noticed. The twins were suddenly hurled aside. The lord's prick was once again erect. He rose and looked the length of her body again; then, like an eagle settling on its prey, he laid himself down between her spread legs. Before she could move or even think of protesting, the thick shaft sank into her and his weight came down upon her, pushing her body into the rough tatami.

She moaned as the thick shaft plunged the length of her unused cunt. The channel parted reluctantly before his charge. At length she could feel rough hairs scratching against the mounds of her ass, still sore at points from the twins' nails. He pulled out suddenly, and she cried out again. He rammed himself full length at her, and his weight drove the breath from her body. This time, however, she began to feel the first intimations of pleasure. Again he pulled back, then slammed his body forward.

His repeated attacks scraped her front against the mats. Her nipples grew erect and painful, and her breasts ached with a dull pain. His motions grew more and more rapid. He scraped his hands the length of her body, and she screamed again. But her channel was moist now, and she felt some of the sensations she had called up when remembering her

34

lovemaking in the nunnery. She moaned with each thrust into her wet interior, and this time there was an element of pleasure in the sound.

Her pleasure seemed to drive the man into a frenzy. He ground his hips into her as if possessed. His hands tore at her back, then at her sides. He lowered his head to her neck and shoulders, sinking his teeth into the soft skin until blood flowed. She cried out in pain and fear, all pleasure gone; then suddenly she felt him erupt in her. Her insides were inundated with a flow of liquid, and his motions became shorter and shorter but no less rough. His entire weight now rested on his hips, and the manroot drilled into her until suddenly he collapsed on her back, his head on her shoulders.

She turned her head to look at the face of her tormentor, now that it was illuminated by a candle as hers was. She trembled at the sight of the face. It had been handsome at one time. Now two scars crossed the face from cheekbones to chin, crossing at the upper lip. The closed eyes opened and looked at her, and she shivered again. The hawk eyes seemed remote and dead.

He rose from her back and regarded her for a moment.

'Untie her and take her out. Have her killed. I've had enough of her.'

Still trembling, she tried to object, but no words would come – only a tiny cry escaped her lips. Her limbs were paralysed, partly by fear, largely because of her confinement. The twins frogmarched her to the sliding door before them, a light of anticipation in their eyes.

As they reached the door he called out after them, 'No – I've changed my mind. Keep her. She's yours.

If she escapes, though, you will pay, like that bitch Oshin.' The prisoner sagged between them in relief.

'In a few months,' added Lord Matsudaira to himself, 'in a few months it will not matter at all. I will not have to hide my pleasures from anyone, especially not my cousins, the Tokugawa.' His high-pitched laughter was the only sound they heard as the three women left his presence.

Chapter 3

The city of Edo stretched out around Goemon and Jiro for what looked like forever. It was the greatest city in the world. The two men, one tall, the other shorter, approached the massive gates of the shogun's castle with trepidation. The massive walls, surrounded by a moat and built in a spiral-enclosed design, loomed massively before them. The gate was set in a large square donjon, topped by a white-walled, tiled guardhouse. They were about to approach one of the low-ranking samurai who, armed with staves, forbade entry to the unbidden, when a figure detached itself from the shadow of the gate. The young samurai, exquisitely dressed, his forehead shaven and shining in the spring sun, bowed to them.

'You are the gentlemen from Miyako. Follow me, please.' Without a word he turned and walked into the castle. As they walked deeper and deeper into the maze, its extent became clear. Far from being a mere castle, it was a veritable city, containing offices and storehouses, barracks, strong points, and still more castles within its nesting walls and moats. They passed men by the hundreds, hurrying to and fro. Many wore the uniforms of low-ranking retainers and samurai of the shogun or of the Tokugawa clan of which he was the head. A few wore the crests of other clans from the great and lesser fiefs across the land. Still fewer were dressed with the opulence of the young exquisite who led Jiro and Goemon. It was a busy administrative quarter, the seat of government of thirty million souls, and the warrior was making way for the bureaucrat.

At each gate or postern their guide would motion to them to wait. He would talk quietly with the commander of the gate's guard, and they would be passed without a question. They walked for what seemed like several miles through the labyrinth. At last they came to an inconspicuous gate in one of the numerous guardhouses. Jiro and Goemon were motioned through, and the door shut rapidly behind them. Both men came to a sudden stop. Four bared swords were aimed at their throats. The silk-clad young samurai who had led them there bowed slightly and disappeared through a sliding door. Behind the four armed men who faced them stood another. He was elderly, and his topknot was grey and wispy, but his stance, brocade robes, and gold sword furnishings bespoke power, wealth, and authority.

He bowed slightly to the two men from Miyako. 'A bath is prepared for you.'

Jiro and Goemon looked at one another with surprise. The offer of the bath was perfectly in order, but the reception that came with it was not. A rack stood ready to receive their swords. Jiro surrendered his long one but kept the shorter wakizashi, or 'guardian of honour.' They followed the elderly man, who had omitted giving his name, down a series of polished wood galleries. Their way was lit by paper windows high up in the walls.

The bathroom was luxurious. The bath full of steaming water was of fragrant cedar. The fittings were of lacquered and gilt brass. They stripped and washed themselves under the eyes of their escort. When they were to dress, they were supplied with formal wear: white silk underkimono tied with a soft sash, grey loose trousers, and a stiff grey surcoat, the shoulders of which were twice as broad as their own. Their hair was made up and oiled by a silent servitor.

At last they were conveyed through another series of rooms and corridors to a small, poorly lit anteroom. The sliding doors before them were guarded by two kneeling samurai in formal wear, both wearing the house crest of the shogun on their breasts. A crack of light shone through the sliding doors, and they could hear a voice, which seemed to be dictating a letter. At last it finished. There was a command.

The old man who had escorted them announced throatily, 'The Presence!' They all bowed low, foreheads to the floor.

'Genpichi, have them advance,' a pleasant voice called out.

Genpichi, Jiro, and Goemon advanced, then knelt and bowed deeply again.

'You may rise.'

Their trunks erect, they faced their sovereign in

all but name, dictator of Japan, the Sei-i-tai shogun, their personal liege lord. The shogun was a hard-faced man of middle age. His hair was greying, and there were lines on his face. He was seated on a low dais, a convenient armrest by his side. The alcove behind him held an antique sword in a gold-and-ivory mounting.

'Miura Jiro.' The shogun looked long and hard at the giant samurai before him; then his gaze swept to Jiro's companion. 'Goemon.' Each bowed as his name was called. The shogun rose. 'I have heard some-what about you from Hanzo. I am interested in good swordsmen and loyal servants.' Abruptly he added, 'Follow me!' and walked to a side door that opened at his approach. 'Genpichi, wait here,' he threw over his shoulder as he walked out. The other two rose hurriedly and followed him.

They followed the shogun across a small canal on an arched bridge. Before them loomed a blank white wall topped by tiles with the Tokugawa crest. Set in the wall was a single heavily riveted door. Before the door stood two samurai. As they saw the three men approaching, the two took a step forward. The shogun motioned Goemon and Jiro to wait, and they stood on the arch of the bridge. The shogun approached the two guards. They stepped aside, their eyes on the two on the bridge, hands hovering near their sword hilts.

One of them knocked his fist against the door. A small spyhole opened at eye level. The shogun whispered at it. The two guards knelt motionless on either side, eyes fixed before them. The iron-studded gate opened. The shogun slipped through and stood on the threshold. He said something in a low voice.

One of the guards called out, 'You may approach.'

Goemon and Jiro stepped through the barred gate, and it closed behind them. They were in a small courtyard. Square paving stones made a path to the side, where a stone lantern overlooked a small washing trough. A single bamboo clump swayed over them. The shogun stood before another door, riveted as the first had been. Jiro turned his head. The gatekeepers were two elderly women. Their faces were lined, but their carriage was erect. They were dressed in cuirasses and light metal head protectors. Each carried two swords and a halberd. They stood perfectly motionless, one to either side of the gate, facing each other.

The shogun called out, 'I am here!' The second gate swung open onto an anteroom. The shogun motioned Jiro and Goemon to follow. They entered the shogun's House of Women. Behind them, the doors closed. The shogun turned and looked at them.

'These precautions are troublesome but necessary. As you can see, I have guards inside, too.'

The two men turned. The gatekeepers were again women, armoured and armed like those outside. But these were distinctly different: They were young girls blooming with youth. The pale pink kimono worn by one, the sleeves and collar of which were visible, contrasted pleasantly with the pale yellow worn by the other. This would be the only opportunity to examine the shogun's women, Jiro decided, and he would do it carefully. He decided that Pink Sleeves was the younger of the two. She had the full, round face and high hairline of the classical Miyako beauty. Her severe expression was belied by the tiny rosebud mouth. Her hair was held

41

high behind her by a gold band. Yellow Robe was thinner, darker than the other, with a smooth, longish face and arching eyebrows.

Goemon, more used to upper-class women, examined their surroundings. The room was a small one. The farther half was a platform of polished and lacquered wood. They stood on a floor of inset black and white river pebbles. A scroll depicting a mythical animal – a lion – hung at his left. At his right hung another scroll, of the crescent moon. At the far end was a sliding fusuma door, lightly painted with images of mountains swathed by clouds in very pale colours. Behind the door Goemon could faintly hear sounds of activity and women's voices.

The shogun dropped his lacquered wooden sandals and stepped up onto the platform. Instead of proceeding, he turned and sat down. He looked steadily at Goemon and Jiro.

'I choose only the best, as you know. These women, for instance' – he indicated the two samurai girls with a wave – 'they are my women but also my samurai. It is good, I think, for all my servants to work harmoniously. I think you should be encouraged to combine your forces. I have heard much of your abilities. I do not want to have my women damaged in any way. So... you may have these women now.' He indicated the two armed guards with his hand and laughed. Without a change of expression he added to the guards, 'Kill them!'

There was no warning, no time to think. Pink Sleeves' halberd, which had stood at her side since the door had been closed, made a whistling arc and flew straight at Jiro's neck. Yellow Robe moved her left hand forward and her right hand back and then stabbed at Goemon with her own pole weapon.

42

Jiro twirled aside to his left. He grasped the wooden shaft of the halberd with his right hand, adding force to the direction the blade was going. He twisted his body to the right and brought the pole forward over his left shoulder and pulled. Rather than fly over with her weapon, the woman samurai let go, and drawing her short sword, she stabbed at Jiro's exposed back. In a flash he had shifted the direction of his torso. He rammed the butt of the halberd into the woman's exposed midriff. She *ooffed* and doubled over. Jiro rose to his feet.

The shogun was laughing. 'Well,' he said in a rough voice, 'what are you waiting for? I said, "Have her."'

Jiro paused for a fraction of a second. Pink Sleeves was trying to stagger away from him and draw her long sword at the same time. There was a whisper. Jiro's short blade leaped from its scabbard. He took a step forward, and the tip of his blade cut up the length of the girl's body, from buttocks to nape. The shogun's jaws clicked together.

Jiro returned his sword to its scabbard in a single movement. The girl struggled to extricate her sword, but suddenly her movements were hampered as the cuirass, its supporting cords cut, fell to the floor with a thud. The back of her kimono parted in a long cut, and the wide sash and ties of her wide trousers, used to hold the swords, parted. The white-skinned, perfectly smooth back was unmarred. Her scabbards fell to the floor. The tops of two plump, pale buttocks appeared, the split between them showing to half its length.

Jiro pulled at his scabbard and loosened the silk cord that secured it in its sash. With several efficient movements he tied the girl's hands behind her back.

Her breath was still coming in harsh grunts, but he knew that if he did not take precautions, she would emasculate, then kill him, with her hands if necessary. The entire fight, from start to finish, had taken less than ten seconds. He held Pink Sleeves by the neck with his left, while his right pulled his cock free. His eyes were held by those of the shogun, who looked on with tolerant amusement.

He felt the smooth plumpness of the girl's ass for a moment. She tried to struggle, but his enormous hand held her still by the nape. The crack of her ass was a warm crevice. His middle finger felt the tiny clenched dot of her asshole and passed on. Through a grove of incredibly soft curls he finally reached her tight hole. Not surprisingly, it was dry, and his questing finger could find no delighting moisture until it penetrated deep into the narrow channel. He worked his finger in and out for a moment. The humidity increased imperceptibly, though the girl shuddered as she tried to avoid the questing finger.

Jiro took his hand away. He had no wish to hurt the girl. To the contrary: He might possibly be the only man, besides the shogun, who would ever have her, and he wanted the memory to be a good one. He filled his mouth with saliva and spat onto his fingers. An intoxicating smell rose to his nostrils and from the digit that had entered her. He moistened it thoroughly, then inserted it again into her orifice. The welcome this time was perceptibly warmer. His finger slid up her channel easily. It slid out again, leaving a trail of saliva, and moved up to the tiny nub of the clitoris. Impatient now, Jiro spread her legs. Unresisting, they parted, and he pushed forward.

She gasped for a moment as she felt the size of his cock. Her lower lips spread as he pushed slowly but

44

inexorably in. Though her channel had been slightly moistened, the penetration caused her some pain. She gasped again, but the battering pressure did not go away. Slowly he slid his engorged cock up the length of her narrow, rubbery insides. He could feel every fold in the tube. It gripped the length of his member with a firm yet yielding grasp.

At last the rough curls at the root of his manhood scraped against her soft ass. They remained there, suspended for a moment in time. He soaked luxuriously in her warmth, she enjoying the unexpected shaft. His fingers remained busy. Gently he tweaked the nubbin of her clitoris, rubbing the fleshy lips over the sensitive button so as not to irritate it. She responded with approval, and tension left her body. He entwined his fingers in the straight beard that hid the lips of her cunt, then rubbed a tiny pinch of hair against the most sensitive spot. Her body jerked in response, and he increased the pressure.

He took a chance and removed his other hand from her neck, sliding it down her body. While one hand supported her hips, the other squeezed her hanging tits, cupping them, then flattening each gently against her ribcage. His hand descended, and he stroked her muscular belly gently. The skin quivered to his touch, and he could hear a slight moan. He felt her smooth ass, slipping his fingers into the crack, then lingering on each perfect mound.

Then both hands were on her hips, and he pulled back. She protested the withdrawal of the feast between her lower lips. He pushed forward once, and she subsided. He withdrew again, and half the length of his shaft, coated with glistening dew, became visible to the sole spectator. Looking down, Jiro examined his prick with satisfaction for a moment, then shoved it back again with satisfaction.

Now he set to work to fuck her in earnest. The movements of his hands and hips were coordinated. He pulled her to him as he shoved his hips forward, withdrawing more slowly. Again and again, at a greater speed, he moved the two of them. The girl was gasping now with expectation and pleasure. Her juices were running freely. A short tremor overcame her, and she came, biting her lip.

But Jiro was not ready yet. His movements became frenzied. He pulled her erect and bit her neck and shoulders. He was too tall for her, and her legs wound around his calves. His hands at her hips supported her body while moving her up and down his slick shaft.

'Ooh, *ooooh!*' she cried, almost senseless with the motion.

Jiro buried his mouth in her neck and closed his eyes as the violence of his own pumping orgasm overcame him. He groaned inarticulately as a flood of creamy liquid rushed the length of his furious pole and inundated the girl before him. His hips ground into her ass carelessly, mashing them almost flat into the bones of his pelvis. He felt as if the top of his head were bursting.

Slowly the spasms died down and the movements ceased. Jiro remembered his friend suddenly. He opened his eyes and looked around in time to see the end of Goemon's affair.

Goemon was too busy with his own problems to follow Jiro's activities. Yellow Robe's thrust was aimed at his belly, and the wooden platform, which ran around three sides of the room, did not allow him room to manoeuvre. He leaped into the air, pulling out a wide purple silk kerchief from the bosom of his robe. The kerchief was part of his disguise as a doctor, and he rarely parted from it. He had held on to it even when dressed in the clothes supplied after the bath.

The kerchief deflected the blow. In a flash, Yellow Robe withdrew her weapon, raised it above her head, and brought it down in a cut at his head. Holding the kerchief in both hands, he tried to deflect the blow, but it was only a feint. The polearm spun, and she cut at his feet. Again he leaped into the air, and she stabbed at him a second time.

This time he managed to loop the kerchief around the shaft of the weapon. Hastily he immobilised the thrust, then leaped in and grabbed at the guard. She dropped her weapon, seized his lapel, turned, and threw him over her head. He fell heavily against the door. She hit at him with the hilt of her great sword. Stunned, he fell to the ground. Almost leisurely, she drew and cut at his supine body. His sweeping kick took her off guard. The sword flew from her grasp as she fell.

They rolled over and over on the ground, neither getting an advantage until Goemon pinned her against the wall. She tried to bite at his neck, but here his knowledge of anatomy was her downfall. His left hand snaked up between their bodies, and his fingers pressed hard against known nerve centres. She struggled for a while, almost dislodging him, until he found the points he wanted in her body that were not covered by armour. With a convulsive effort, he struck at those spots in succession. She went limp, paralysed by the pressure. Goemon

47

breathed heavily and rolled off her. He looked up. The other girl was standing bent over, her kimono dangling on the floor. Jiro's powerful frame was driving his stiff cock steadily into her. Goemon could see the girl's face. Sweat beaded her forehead, and her eyes were almost closed. Her breath was coming in whimpers, which seemed to be of a rising pleasure. The shogun's eyes now turned to Goemon, and he turned back to his own affairs.

The girl lay on the pebbled floor at his feet. Effortlessly – she weighed much less than Rosamund – he picked her up and laid her on the wooden floor. He knew he had little time before the paralysis wore off, and he swiftly stripped the girl of her armour and clothing and stripped himself. He spread her unresisting legs and positioned himself on his knees between them. He considered for a moment, then took the girl's wrists and bent them behind and under her. Plump breasts tipped with dark brown, erect nipples stared at him, forced up by her arched back. He ran his tongue slowly over one, and then the other, then bit each in turn gently. He sucked hungrily at them in turn, forcing first one and then the other as deeply as he could into his mouth.

The girl tried feebly to struggle, but the effect of Goemon's blows slowed her movements. Still holding her wrists behind her, he moved backward. His tongue, plentifully moistened by saliva, drew a track down the middle of her chest. He paused a while at the well of her belly button, leaving a moist round pucker. His chin grazed the forest of crisp black hairs, and he took a few in his teeth and tugged at them. His lower lip reached the beginning of her lower lips, and he moved his head right and left, teasing the two rolls of flesh. His mouth moved lower, and he fixed onto the tiny drenched button of her clitoris. His tongue teased at it for a moment or two, rolling over and under it, moistening it as roughly as he could with his oral digit. Then he plunged hungrily into her narrow opening. His tongue pushed in as far as it could go, and his lips covered as much of hers as he could.

She began to react to the treatment. Her ass jerked up, and through the thighs that blocked his ears, Goemon fancied he could hear a muted moaning. He dug furiously into her, trying to be careful but nipping her tender flesh inadvertently with his teeth. The moisture was coming hard and free now, and his lower face was covered. Now she was holding him with her thighs, and her imprisoned hands seemed to be begging to be let loose for other reasons than to kill him. Much as he wanted to, Goemon could not let go, knowing that as a samurai she would obey her master's command even in the throes of her pleasure.

She came in an explosive climax that almost wrenched her hands out of his grip and drenched his face with musky dew. Before the spasms had died down, he was on his knees between her legs. His fleshy sword penetrated her flooded channel easily, gliding up the length of her cunt. Her legs gripped him convulsively. Unable to move her hands, she stroked his strong thighs and buttocks with her feet and calves.

At first his movements were controlled and regular. Looking down into her sweaty face, he licked her lips, her neck and her shoulders. His mouth dipped lower, and by pulling on her arms, he brought her tits to greater prominence and sucked and lightly bit the nipples. As his own pleasure rose in his balls, his strokes became harder and less controlled. He rammed himself furiously home as his cream erupted the length of his prick and flooded her glowing channel. Her legs clutched at him once again convulsively, and they both collapsed in exhausted satisfaction. Goemon looked up from his companion just in time to see his friend climax too.

The shogun looked from one couple to the other. 'Very impressive. Dress yourselves and follow me.' He turned to the two guards. 'These men are now under my protection. You have done well. You will attend me tonight. Tell the majordomo.'

The girls, who had rolled to their knees when he addressed them, bowed in gratitude. Goemon's last look at them as he followed the shogun and Jiro through the door was of two rounded sets of buttocks and sweaty backs poking up in the air.

They sat in a small wooden-floored room high in a tower that crowned the shogun's innermost haven.

'Matsudaira Konosuke, you have replaced your father well.'

Goemon bowed at the compliment.

'I have need of strong and reliable men who will serve me. Men who are not afraid of unconventionality and who fear nothing. You will serve as my agents.'

The two men bowed their thanks with a loud 'Hai!' acknowledging their acquiescence.

'You, Lord Matsudaira,' the shogun continued, 'how peaceful is this land?'

Goemon's eyebrows rose. 'Very peaceful. We have had no disturbances since...' he did not complete the sentence.

'"Since Osaka," you were about to say,' the shogun grunted. 'Would it surprise you to know that is not necessarily true? We are faced with a difficult situation. We rule this land in the way my august father planned. Superficially, it appears the wars are over. In reality as you know, we, the Tokugawa clan, do not have absolute control. We must compromise; sometimes we must bargain. We must rely on allies, such as you, the Matsudaira clans, our cousins. This is all as it should be. But one of our greatest strengths is the sense of unity in this land, which was so torn by war only some years ago. We are afraid that if news of unrest were to spread, more unrest would follow.'

The two men nodded in agreement. Jiro was puzzled. He still could not see what the shogun was driving at.

The shogun continued, 'I want you to help me quell unrest – quietly, so that no news of the unrest or the quelling of it should get out.' He paused and looked at Jiro's uncomprehending face. 'You have a question?'

'What is to stop the Presence from simply arresting such culprits and executing them?'

A shadow of impatience passed momentarily over the shogun's face. 'First,' he said, 'it must be done quietly. Some clans such as Mori and Satsuma, which fought against us in the past, might still try to rise, and our mandate from the All under Heaven is to keep the peace. Second, we suspect that highly placed individuals might be concerned, and we must preserve the semblance of harmony within the court and the ruling clan, both here and in Miyako. I do not want anyone to come to trial. And third, the southern barbarians are knocking on our gates, as you well know.'

Goemon moistened his lips. So his relationship with Rosamund was an open secret. Well, that did not matter so long as the fiction of secrecy was maintained.

'Some of these barbarians are plain merchants, but others peddle their religion, which in other lands has served as a forerunner of invasion. I will not allow the same to happen here. Do what you must to keep it discreet.' He looked meaningfully at Goemon, who gave him a bland look back.

'Lord Matsudaira!' Goemon straightened at the new tone that had entered his liege's voice. 'You shall be our agent. We have been informed that several individuals have been plotting to overthrow our government. They centre around the city of Miyako. One of them is a merchant of Osaka, name unknown; a second is a high-ranking noble. They plan to meet in Miyako in the near future to plot their nefarious scheme. Stop them. Miura Jiro will be your assistant, and you may appoint others as you need them.'

They bowed again with a throaty *'Hai!'*

The shogun indicated two cloth-wrapped parcels, a small square one and a longer bundle, both resting on raised lacquered trays. 'These are yours. Use them when necessary.'

Goemon and Jiro bowed again, and the shogun rose and left the room.

They rose from their bows and looked at one another. Goemon bowed towards the tray and lifted the small parcel. It was a flat lacquered box threaded with a cord for tying to a sash. On it was the Tokugawa crest in gold. Inside was a single folded sheet of paper. It bore a familiar word in black,

'Obey!' stamped with the shogun's red seal. Goemon tucked the box into the folds of his robe. The long bundle contained a pair of swords in exquisite mountings. The blades were of the finest workmanship. The hilts were white sharkskin and twisted white silk cord, and the sheaths were white-and-gold buffed lacquer. He raised the pair re-

An elderly maid led them through silent corridors and passed them on to a male guide, who passed them on to another until, the two found themselves in a room with the clothes they had entered with.

'Well, what now?' Jiro had had time to regain his poise. Unused to all the luxury of the shogun's palace, he wished to return to more familiar surroundings. 'There are lots of merchants in Osaka. Where do we start, Goemon?'

Goemon refused to meet his friend's eyes. At last he said with a sigh, 'It's true there are many merchants in Osaka – it is a merchant city, after all – but I think there is one in particular who may be involved. I'm afraid I shall have to search him out.'

Jiro suddenly remembered the tea merchant Saizo, who had befriended Goemon years before. He nodded sympathetically. Goemon had long since told him of his suspicion that Saizo had been a part of the anti-Tokugawa forces during the Osaka war.

'We will have to go to Osaka. That is the first strand of the thread. We may as well tell Rosamund and Okiku. They, too, may be of assistance. You had better go to Miyako to tell them.'

Jiro nodded. 'I don't know any Osaka merchants, but I'll also keep my eyes open for any lord who might be coming to Miyako. I might find out something. We'll take a ship back to Osaka and proceed from there to Miyako by road.'

Chapter 4

Osaka bustled with commercial life. The city had emerged as a commercial centre only in the previous century. Denied political supremacy by its rival Edo, it concentrated all its energy on trade.

Jiro walked wonderingly through the city. Samurai were of less account here than merchants, and his two swords seemed to make less impression than Goemon's subdued merchant's silks. They threaded their way through stone warehouses and wooden booths. At one point their passage was blocked by a mass of people intent on a parade that passed before their eyes.

'What is it?' Jiro asked angrily.

A craftsman eyeing the two-sworded giant respectfully cringed a bit but answered, 'Southern barbarians! They are going to meet with the magistrate!' He bowed perfunctorily and turned to watch the show.

Goemon sucked in his breath as he watched the

foreigners pass. He had his own personal southern barbarian and felt he had a standard for comparison. None of those who passed by looked like Rosamund. They were short, swarthy men with long, pointed beards and moustaches. They dressed in baggy, colourful pantaloons, tight jerkins, and short cloaks. Some wore broad-rimmed plumed hats and carried swords; others, obviously their servants, held parasols to shade their masters.

At their head strode one who attracted the most attention. He was dressed more richly than his followers, and a vulgar gold chain hung around his neck. The hilt of his rapier bore a yellow jewel, and the cup that served as guard was enamelled and inlaid. It was his size and colour that impressed the watchers. The man towered over his companions, and his scowling face was a dark brown, darker even than the skin of a labourer. Goemon could not help grinning as he saw Jiro look loweringly at the foreign giant. No doubt his friend was contemplating the outcome of a duel with an opponent of apparently his own size and strength.

The group of foreigners passed, and the crowd dispersed. The two men found a small noodle stall.

'Wait here,' said Goemon. 'I must talk to him alone.'

Jiro nodded. 'Should I come in if you're not out soon?'

'No. There'll be no trouble. He doesn't know who I am, and perhaps I will later suggest that you, being masterless, will join his plot.' His voice was sad as he said it. Saizo, a tea merchant of Osaka, had saved him from drowning, had brought him into his home, and had even offered to adopt him. Before adopting the occupation of merchant, Goemon suspected,

Saizo had been the spymaster for Sanada Yukimura, commander of the anti-Tokugawa forces in the Osaka war. Now old ghosts would crop up to trouble both men as they went about their duty.

The door to the shop was uncharacteristically shut. Memories from his employment in the house as a clerk surfaced, and Goemon turned down a side alley. He knocked lightly at an inconspicuous door. A wrinkled female face peered at him as the door opened. Noting his features, the elderly servant woman opened the door and bowed at him, tears in her eyes.

'Master Goemon! You have been gone for so long! Oh, oh! ... And to return at such a sad time ...'

'What has happened? Tell me – is the master all right?'

'He is dying. He has had a sickness for the past few weeks, and he is dying. The doctors have given up. Perhaps you ... but you are probably no longer a doctor. I have offered prayers to the kannon, to the kami, to the ancestors, but nothing helps. The master is dying.'

Quickly Goemon made his way through the wooden corridors to Saizo's bedroom. Saizo lay there surrounded by members of his family. The attending physician fussed with his vials and drugs, but it was clear there was little to be done. The patient's face was sunken, his lips were dry, and his skin was marred by large purple blotches.

'Do you know what it is?' Goemon asked of the doctor, after identifying himself as a former employee.

The doctor shook his head. 'No. I have never seen the like. Perhaps he got the disease through his association with foreigners. I have never seen the like.'

Goemon hurried to bow by his former employer's pallet. Saizo's eyes opened a trifle. His eyelids twitched and quivered slightly at the sight of Goemon's concerned face. He tried to raise himself, then sank back on the pillows. He whispered something, and the senior clerk elbowed Goemon aside and bent an ear to his master's mouth. Saizo whispered again. The clerk tried to protest but was silenced fiercely by the dying man.

'The master would like to talk to... to master Goemon. Alone.'

Protesting but obedient, the household members left the room. Saizo's sons and concubine were the last to go, casting questioning glances at Goemon. Saizo watched them go, his breath coming in gasps. As soon as the sliding fusuma doors were closed, he stretched out a hand and pulled Goemon to him.

'Goemon, I am glad you are here. I need your help.' His voice was hard and clear, much like the voice of the Saizo Goemon had known before, not at all like the sick man he was now.

Goemon bowed. 'Anything in my power...'

'I must leave Osaka, and dying was the most convenient way. You have come back in time. I doubt if you can take back the place you left, but at least you can help me. Be at the mortuary of the Saionji temple, here in the tea merchants' quarter, at night. Release me from my coffin.'

Comprehension swept through Goemon. 'Then you're not dying?'

'No. Nonsense. It's just time I left, and there are some other reasons...'

Goemon thought he knew what those reasons were. He said nothing. It was best, he thought, to play along in hope of learning more. It seemed, he thought sadly, that he had indeed come to the right place. His old master was indeed the 'merchant of Osaka' involved in the plot. He bowed again.

'Tonight without fail,' whispered the older man in parting.

The household filed in again just as Saizo went into paroxysms. He gasped for air and arched his back, and his eyes rolled in his head. Then suddenly the fit was over, and he fell back onto the silk pallet. The doctor administered restoratives, then massaged the hand and then the chest, but nothing was of avail. Saizo the tea merchant was dead.

Goemon left, unnoticed in the ensuing commotion.

Few people linger by mortuaries at night. Goemon and Jiro were unremarked as they climbed the wall and broke into the wooden building. There was one single barrel-like round coffin in the hall. Carefully, so as not to disturb the outside appearance of the coffin, they pried off the lid. Saizo was curled up inside, head lolling by his chest. In the light of the single lantern they carried, his skin had the fish-white pallor of death.

Jiro bent forward and with all his giant strength hauled out the body. It was cold and smelled somehow unpleasant. They laid it on the floor, and Jiro wondered whether they were perhaps too late. The old man might have died of suffocation by now.

Goemon bent by the body and whispered, 'Saizo! Saizo!' There was no response, and Goemon again called his former master's name. This time there was a faint flutter. Saizo started moving his limbs; eventually his eyes opened and he regarded Goemon in the light of the muffled lantern. He breathed evenly for a while, then motioned them to help him to his feet. Jiro bent down and picked him up, and the three left the mortuary silently.

There was a small grove in the precints of a nearby shrine. They sat in a circle and conferred.

'Goemon,' said Saizo, 'your arrival was blessed by the gods. I must tell you something, then depart. I have never told a soul, but years ago I served with a very select group of men in the Osaka war. Unfortunately, we lost, and my master and friends perished in the firing of the castle. Since then, I have become a tea merchant.

'Politics was never my interest,' he went on, 'so with the death of my master, I had no compunction in supporting, or at least being neutral, to the Tokugawa regime. But in the past few months, someone has learned that I was once on the other side. They, or he, has been trying to pressure me to join in opposing the government. I gather their plans are violent, whereas I have had enough violence for a lifetime.

'Although I do not love the Tokugawa, I do care for my peace and quiet and that of my family. That is why I decided to die in the most convincing way possible. I can now go off and wander a bit, and my family and business will remain unthreatened.'

'Who is trying to pressure you? Perhaps my friend can convince him to leave you alone.'

Saizo smiled up at Jiro's bulk, looking beside him. 'Master Jiro reminds me of a monk I once knew. Anyway, you had best stay away from Rokuro. He is a dangerous man and in any case no concern of yours.'

'Perhaps not. Still...'

Saizo shot a sharp glance in Goemon's direction. 'Well, you've always been a deep one. I don't know what your interest in the matter is. As for me, I want out of it. And if you'll take an old man's advice, one who's played soldier often enough, you'll leave these things alone.'

'Who is this Rokuro?' persisted Goemon.

'He's a merchant, mainly rice and sake, which means he is very wealthy. He deals a lot with the foreigners – the Chinese and the southern barbarians – though he hates them all, I think. I can't stand the fellow; still, as a tea merchant I had to do business with him. He has much business in the Chinese quarter and imports much from them too.'

He looked slyly at Goemon. 'He is putting together a consortium to offer some high-class goods to the court of the All under Heaven. He invited me to join the consortium, and I made a vague pretence of agreeing. I've even gone through the motions of collecting the goods – some of my best teas.'

'Why are you so reluctant?' asked Goemon sharply.

'Because he hinted that there's more to it than that and because his hints had an unpleasant smell of ... undesirable pressure, let us say, based on my past.'

Goemon chewed his lip. 'If I could get into that consortium...'

'Easily. The founding meeting is to be held the day after tomorrow, at an inn here in Osaka.'

'How can I go without authorisation? I'm no longer your clerk.'

'Unfortunately, no. However, if you are determined, there is nothing simpler. I'll write a

60

document authorising you as my agent, and you'll present it to him. I'll even write a withdrawal order from my warehouse if you wish.'

Goemon sighed and slapped his thigh. 'That won't do, as you well know. We'd need your seal, and your heir has that by now.'

The old man coughed delicately. 'Well, that's not completely accurate. In my former profession I had many occasions to use duplicate seals. The habit never really left me.' His hand darted into his robe and procured a small, flat box.

In the moonlight, Saizo wrote out the orders confirming Goemon as his agent and sealed them with his square red seal. Before they parted for the last time he added some words: 'Goemon, I don't know what you are up to, and I am not interested. I only request that you do no harm to my house and heirs. I wish you luck in your enterprise, whatever it is. Anyway, now I must go. I'll be heading north. A wandering monk on the lonely road to the north is never amiss.'

They bowed in farewell, and Saizo vanished into the dark.

The Chinese quarter differed in some undefinable way from the rest of the city. The Chinese merchants, disdainful of local culture, had brought as much of their own with them as they could. Men in long gowns and peculiar headgear strolled the narrow streets. The shops smelled of different spices, and even the architecture was slightly unfamiliar. Like all men far from home, the Chinese merchants brought with them their small, familiar comforts.

Jiro and Goemon stopped at a teashop, the last in a long string of such stops in various places around the city. Goemon was relearning a former trade as fast as he could. And they were gathering a respectable amount of information about city merchants, including Rokuro. While they drank a fragrant tea, Goemon idly questioned the waiter, who, though not a Chinese, seemed to have adopted many of their mannerisms and all of their dress. Goemon praised the tea, as an ex-clerk in a tea business. He soon found himself deep in conversation with the waiter, then with the proprietor. Since it was midmorning, customers were few, and the man was an eager talker. Jiro sat impassively in the corner, watching the passage of people in the street. He was hot and, he realised, horny. The boat passage from Edo had made him bored and restless, and he wondered when he would get home again.

The conversation shifted to pleasures other than tea, and Goemon ventured a question. 'Ah, I remembered there was a splendid girl here once. Chu Hsi-men introduced me to her. Her name was Willow Girl . . .'

The proprietor and the waiter both professed ignorance of the name. 'Though if you wish to find her,' added the owner, 'the Floating World bailiff lives not far from here. Of course, there are other delights you might wish to sample . . .'

Goemon wound down the conversation at length, and they took their leave. As they walked down a narrow street, a movement before them drew Goemon's attention. A hired palanquin had stopped. A woman emerged from it and, with one quick step, was swallowed by the entrance. The palanquin bearers shouldered their conveyance and trotted off. Something about the movement that tickled Goemon's memory . . .

'Jiro, stop a moment,' he ordered. He looked at the house, wondering whether he had ever been there before. It was a plain commoner's house, fronting the street. The main door was closed, but a small wicket was cut into the lacquered wooden slab, so that one could enter with a bent head and hunched posture. The sight of the house did not stir any memories. They were about to pass on, when the strains of a biwa lute floated through the entryway.

Goemon's face lit up. 'That's it!' he said. 'The biwa player! She was the one we just saw. Now, what was her name? ...'

Jiro, bewildered, could only follow his friend as the smaller man stepped through the open doorway into a gloomy, packed earth-floored hall. Bent nearly double to pass through the door, Jiro straightened in time to hear Goemon call out, 'Forgive me for bothering you!' He repeated the call again when there was no answer. This time the playing of the biwa stopped for a moment; then it resumed, but there was also the sound of feet walking on wood.

An old, harsh-faced woman with the tiniest feet Jiro had ever seen bowed to them from the end of the hall. 'Yes? What is it you want, please?' Her Japanese was almost unaccented but had a strange singing quality.

Goemon, who had been expecting someone else to emerge, was slightly taken aback. 'Ah ... forgive me for bothering you while you are busy, but ... ah ... some years ago I met a charming young lady, Willow Girl by name, and I wondered if I might pay her a visit.'

'There is no Willow Girl here!' snapped the old woman. She was about to add something, when she was interrupted by a voice that called something out to her in a foreign language. She answered in kind, then muttered roughly, 'Wait a minute. Someone will see you.'

A few minutes later they were greeted by the lute player herself, still holding the ivory pick. She was a plump, short girl. Her face was smooth and almost round. Delicate arched eyebrows outlined humorous-looking eyes. Her hair was held in a series of buns close by her head, one over each ear and one at the back. Her figure under the robes she wore appeared rounded and plump as her cheeks. Her feet, encased in red felt shoes, were even smaller, Jiro decided, than the old woman's.

'Yes, honoured sirs? How may I serve you?' Her tone implied that the question was rhetorical.

Goemon smiled in recognition. He still could not recall the girl's name, but she had accompanied Willow Girl while the latter danced. He bowed.

'I believe we have met before. Several years ago I had the honour to be entertained here by you and a friend, Willow Girl. I trust she is well?'

The girl creased her forehead in thought. 'I'm afraid I can't remember at the moment. Willow Girl, lucky woman, has returned to the Central Kingdom as the third concubine of merchant Chu.' She smiled impishly. 'But if you would care to step inside, I am sure I will remember you soon enough...' Her invitation was clear.

Her eyes slid to Jiro, and she giggled. 'I would undoubtedly have remembered your friend, though. Would you, too, join us? I'm afraid that at the moment all my maids are out...'

Jiro bowed his thanks and murmured his acceptance, and both men followed the girl as she swayed before them into the gloom of the house.

She brought them to a room that was furnished in the Chinese style, with several tables and uncomfortable-looking high-backed chairs, a few scattered tabourets, and an arched doorway that looked out onto a small garden. A curtain covered one side of the room, and Goemon knew that a bed lay behind that.

Gracefully she offered them seats, relieved Jiro of his long sword, and called for tea and candied fruits. Goemon's practised merchant's eyes noted that the fittings were wearing thin and the furnishings were old, indicating decline in its first stages. His eyes shifted to the girl who stood quietly before them, smiling all the while.

'Shall I play for you gentlemen?' she asked, indicating the lute that stood by the wall.

Goemon chuckled in memory. 'You are a wonderful player. As I remember, you also play the flute quite well too.'

The girl laughed shyly in response.

'You speak very good Japanese now. When I first met you, you did not speak it at all...'

Memory lit the girl's face. 'Of course! You are the first Japanese gentleman I had. You are a tea merchant.' She laughed delightedly. 'So you are back after so many years to pick another peach?'

The clue she had given him reminded him of her name, Peach Blossom, and he gave an appropriate Chinese quotation in reply.

She laughed delightedly, and Jiro joined in with another saying.

'I am sorry I cannot offer you one of my maids,' she repeated, 'but they are all out. I have been out too, to the public bath. Perhaps, nonetheless, I can

65

do my poor best for both of you together?'

Jiro's eyes lit up, and Goemon bowed in reply. 'At our previous meeting,' he said, 'I had the honour of pleasing you and a friend. Allow me to reciprocate.'

'No, no!' She bowed bashfully. 'You do me the honour.' She slid forward from her seat on the tabouret before them to kneel on the floor, and knocked her head several times in a deep bow to the floor before them. She rose slightly and slid her hands the length of their legs to their laps. Her busy plump hands flipped aside their robes and exposed their two erect cocks.

'They are very beautiful,' she said reverently.

She leaned forward and kissed each erect member. Her trained lips nibbled lightly at the heads, lifted the flanges of each shaft in turn. Like a plump bee she sipped the transparent, sticky liquor that appeared at each tip. Her fingers gently scratched the hairy bags below. Then she rubbed the length of the shafts, smoothing the skin so delicately that Jiro had a hard time restraining himself from grabbing her then and there.

She smiled at them, her eyes upturned to see their faces.

'You are so very nice,' she said. 'Some of the Japanese gentlemen who come here are a trifle impatient.'

She rose from her squat, dropping her under-trousers as she did so. For a short second she held her robe open, disclosing the tiny bush that hid her jade gate. Then her hands rose as she dropped the hem and stepped out of the undergarment. She parted her bodice slightly, showing the smooth upper curve of her breasts.

As she bent over them to pour more tea, Jiro and

Goemon looked long at her hidden charms. Peach Blossom slid a hand into the collar of each man, and leaning forward once again to afford them a sight of her breasts, she licked Jiro's ear, then Goemon's. She retreated again, this time pulling both men with her. They rose at her bidding.

The three of them walked to the curtained side of the room. Their hands were around her waist, Jiro, who was on her right, had his left hand in the crack of her cunt. Her bound feet made her sway as she walked, and the swaying increased the friction of his digit, which was soon oily with her juices.

Goemon on her right held one of her plump, nubile tits in his hand. He rolled the nipple between thumb and finger, urging the little nubbin on to greater lengths.

Her own hands she slid along the hard buttocks of her men. Following the cracks, her fingers wandered lower. Because of the differences in their heights, she could easily slip her soft hands between their legs as they took the few steps until she was feeling the heavy, full bags that hung in front. The three of them stood for a while feeling and touching. At last she whispered, 'Sit down, please, side by side.'

They twitched aside the curtain that hid a bed alcove, and the two men did as she had bidden. She looked at their erect machines for a long moment, then knelt between them again. She held on to both cocks, then with a rapid motion leaped forward and licked the length of Goemon's pole. His hips jerked. Before he could react in any other fashion, she turned her head and repeated the motion with Jiro. Back to Goemon; then Jiro again. With each lick she leaned farther forward, until the men's knees were bearing the full weight of her torso. Her soft, pendant breasts tickled the hairy joints and excited them on.

She rested for a moment on her heels and looked at their faces. Jiro was the one she chose. With a smooth motion she rose to her feet and climbed onto his lap. He had a momentary glimpse of the hair-covered slit, and then his cock was engulfed in the moist, hungry warmth of her cunt. She settled herself comfortably, leaned forward, and sucked the entire length of Goemon's rampant prick into her mouth.

Her clever tongue tickled the length of Goemon's shaft while one hand supported his hairy balls carefully. Her nails scratched softly at the corrugations and bumps in the bag. She moved her head up and down, and his scrotum tightened involuntarily.

She raised her smooth ass high so that Jiro, who had leaned back, could see the length of the dark crack between her full-moon mounds. He could barely see the tiny rosebud of her rear hole and the hairless lips of her cunt sucking supplicatingly on the broad head of his cock. She grasped the shaft and churned its length round and round in her cunt. He sighed involuntarily, and his hips jerked forward. With exquisite slowness she settled down the length of the shaft, while at the same time drawing Goemon's prick into the warm cavern of her mouth.

Goemon slid his hands under her and clenched his fists over her breasts. She gave a small cry of protest at the harshness of his grip. He relented, and his fingers supported them with more concern. He stroked the swollen nipples, pulled the breasts together, and pinched the sensitive under skin lightly. In approval she hummed around his prick, which vibrated in sympathy.

Meanwhile, Jiro was not idle. He spread her ass mounds and explored her ass with his large hands. They were plump and well rounded, and he took his time, stroking the smooth skin while her cunt jigged up and down the length of his shaft. A searching finger found her clenched asshole. He wet it first at the fountain of her dew-bedecked cunt, then inserted the digit questioningly into her rear entrance. After a slight resistance, it opened for him, and he thrust the length forward into a warm, clenching darkness.

The slow mutual explorations quickened as all three felt their desire overcoming them. Jiro's hand became more demanding, trying to force her down onto his cock and his searching finger. Goemon's hips started to jerk uncontrollably, ramming the length of his fleshy spear into the depths of her mouth. Her tongue flicked longingly at the length, and her ass ground heavily into Jiro's lap. They were all trembling now with the effort and the tension.

Peach Blossom tasted the first spurts of Goemon's fluid as preliminary drops erupted from the tip of his prick. Goemon's climax rose from his balls with a rush. He arched his hips uncontrollably, uncaring of the effect on her receiving mouth. Ready for him, she controlled the thrust with her free hand. She swallowed the hot, slick fluid as it gushed into her mouth and flooded her tongue. At the same time, feeling her own climax, she ground her hips down onto Jiro. His large hands clamped at her soft buns, and he panted heavily as his own seed splashed her interior in a massive eruption.

She raised her head at last from Goemon's diminished member. With a courteous 'By your leave,' she raised her ass from Jiro's soaking lance.

She swayed over to a small table, her smooth, plump buns rotating in enticing curves. The backs of her thighs glistened with moisture. She walked slowly back, giving the men time to savour the sight of her jouncing breasts and dripping bush. She held a small lacquered tray with steaming towels. Kneeling between Jiro and Goemon, who had sprawled back on the bed, she handed a warm, steaming towel to each of them. Gratefully each one spread the towel on his sweating face and wiped it vigorously. Meanwhile she applied other towels and gently wiped each man's lolling cock.

When they were all more comfortable, she nestled between them. Her busy hands played with their bodies, stroking strong chest muscles, lightly pinching male nipples, diddling both cocks or treasuring their pendulous bags. In the meantime she chattered on, talking about the weather, amusing events in Osaka, the flowers in her garden.

Lazily Jiro traced a circle around a plump areola. 'So beautiful,' he said.

She smiled up at him. 'Yes. Some men appreciate them very much. Others prefer other parts ...' She giggled. 'Some don't seem to prefer anything at all. There are some very strange men – at least to me, a foreigner, they seem strange ... Do you know, I met a man some time ago who wore makeup constantly!'

'Makeup?' asked Goemon indifferently. 'A mountebank or actor of some sorts? There is a new form of entertainment that has become popular among the lower classes called, if I remember, "kuuki," no doubt because it is very windy.' He laughed and added confidently, 'The authorities will ban it soon.'

'Well, he was very strange,' continued the girl.

Jiro's prick had returned to life under her ministrations, and she was filling in the time until she could go on with her real business. 'He wore a hat, which is unusual here but common and proper at home. His face was painted, and he didn't join in the fun at all. You see, I was invited to dance at a party at the home of a merchant, Rokuro. He sat behind a screen, and after seeing me dance and sing, he took a fancy to me and invited me behind the screen to entertain him.' She curled over and kissed Goemon's rising prick. 'But he was nothing like you, my dear. No imagination whatsoever. And ever so pompous. All he wanted was for me to sit on his lap while he smacked me with the board he carried. That was rather nice, but he had chewed the tip, and it was all splinters.' She giggled again and transferred her kisses to Goemon's balls, while rolling Jiro's prick back and forth on his belly.

Both men were breathing hard now. Ignoring their emotions, she continued. 'No, he was not very nice. Sooo serious, as if the world rested on his shoulders. I jogged on him, and his brocade robe was too stiff for comfort. I wanted to take it off, but he refused. He said he was comfortable, and in any case, he preferred azaleas around him.' She made a wry face, then turned and kissed Jiro's ear, which caused him to jump and reach for her hips.

'What did he mean, he preferred azaleas around him?' asked Goemon, stroking her spine.

'Oh, it was a joke, you see. It seems his wife's name is Azalea, and the interior of his villa was painted by some famous artist with pictures of azaleas in bloom, and by coincidence his robe was embroidered with azalea blooms.' She raised herself on an elbow and looked down the length of their three bodies.

'I see you gentlemen would honour me again,' she said in a surprised tone. Jiro grinned and reached for her, but she evaded his hands. She threw a plump thigh over Goemon's supine form and slid the lips of her cunt up and down the length of his cock. Then, raising herself on her knees, she impaled herself slowly on the burning lance.

Goemon felt the pleasure of penetrating slowly into her engulfing twat. The walls of her channel clung together stickily, parting only reluctantly as he probed deeper. Manfully he restrained himself from hurrying the process. He was snorting and shivering by the time her ass rested on his thighs. She rested there for a moment, then raised herself slowly until the entire length of his cock was exposed. Then she hurriedly plunged the entire length into herself again.

Jiro rose and knelt at Goemon's head. The shorter man had a full view of his friend's hairy, pendulous balls and erect shaft. The tip of Jiro's shaft glistened for a moment before Peach Blossom's dark oval of a mouth descended and hid the sight.

She licked and sucked at the tremendous member for a few seconds. Jiro, on his knees, started jerking his hips forward. She grasped the shaft and disengaged. Still kneeling forward so her breasts tickled Goemon's chest, she smiled at the giant.

'There is another way, most pleasing if you care to try it?' She wriggled her rump, and Jiro smiled.

Jiro knelt behind her and admired the sight of Goemon's balls sprouting from between her two perfect moons. She grasped Jiro's cock shaft and aimed him accurately at her nether hole as he parted her plump hillocks. He leaned forward, and she

72

controlled his entry. The length of his magnificent maleness sank slowly and pleasurably into her tight, slick anus.

When both men were well inside her, Peach Blossom sighed. The men could feel one another's length through the girl's slick inner tissues. Their balls rubbed together and against her smooth skin. She closed her eyes in pleasure, then moved her hips in a wriggling motion.

'I'm yours, gentlemen – all yours,' she said in a small voice. 'I cannot help you. Please help yourselves. Do not think of me, I beg you. Merely conduct yourselves as you wish.' She bowed down, her face buried in Goemon's neck.

For a moment, Jiro paused. Then he pulled back slowly and poised himself at the entrance to her hole. The hood of his erection widened the hole painfully, and she lay perfectly still, awaiting their pleasure. He rammed forward with all his weight as Goemon arched his hips against the onslaught. Both Goemon and the girl grunted with effort – she as the two pricks penetrated her before and behind, Goemon as the double weight came down upon him. She could feel the two rigid rods rubbing together inside her. She butted her head against Goemon's neck in pleasure. Jiro retreated and rammed again, as Goemon tried to emulate his friend beneath her.

They shook her between them, both powerful bodies pummelling her delicate plump one between them. Jiro started a sideways jerking movement that sent shivers down her spine as her ass and cunt were fully assaulted by the power of her men. She groaned with the pleasure of the assault, held immobile as a puppet. Jiro and Goemon competed in exploring her body with their hands. Four hands

73

squeezed her tits and teased her nipples, stroked her haunches and thighs, scratched her back, and stroked her neck and ears. All three of them were gasping with pleasure while the powerful stroking became faster and faster.

All three of them paused for a moment on the peak. Jiro's prick was rammed well up her backside, and Goemon's prick was tickling the entrance to her cervix when the first spurts from the men started inundating her. Jiro shook with the power of his orgasm, and his rutting energy transmitted itself through Peach Blossom's nerve endings and tissues to Goemon, who exploded in turn as her cunt clenched over his prick and her ass muscles clenched over Jiro's.

The liquid spurts pumped deeply into her, and the streams of liquid ran out and flooded the inter-mingled pubic hairs and overflowed onto the bedspread. At last they collapsed together, lying side by side, still joined at their loins, all three breathing deeply.

'Well?' asked Goemon as they walked away from the Chinese quarter.

'Superb,' answered his friend. 'We shall have to teach Okiku and Rosamund some of her tricks.'

'They'll kill us if we tell them we had fun without them.'

'And had to pay for it as well! We shall have to send an appropriate gift to redeem my tobacco box and your netsuke toggle. They have our crests...'

'Well, let's do that quietly once we return to Miyako. I'll have to give some extra writing lessons, I imagine, to earn the sum, and I'll have to hide it from Okiku, but it was worth it.'

74

Goemon poked his giant friend in the ribs. 'I introduced you; I'll pay the tab. They'll never know. I'll hide it in official accounts, under Information Received from Agents.' His voice turned serious. 'I hope you were not too besotted to note the information she gave us.'

'I didn't want to bring attention to the matter, though I assumed you'd noticed,' answered Jiro with asperity.

'We're going to have to split up. I will fulfill Saizo's commission with this Rokuro character. You must return to Miyako. I don't know how, but you must find this azalea lover. I feel more and more sure that we are on the track of our man.

Chapter 5

The house was spotlessly clean, and Okiku wondered what else she could do with her time. Jiro had been gone for almost a month. She could not help wondering what the shogun wanted from him and Goemon. It was growing dark. Outside the modest dwelling, which befitted a successful teacher, the sounds of day faded, and the rustle of straw sandals and clack of wooden ones seemed to die off. She saw the young maid contemplating herself in the shiny lacquered surface of a wooden chest.

Okiku looked at the maid critically. She was a plump farmgirl from the outskirts of Miyako. She had been sent by a friend who owed a small debt to Jiro. She wondered what Jiro would see in this young thing. Artlessly, her rounded cheeks and rosebud mouth emphasising her youth, the maid posed before her reflection. Nice fat ass, thought Okiku lazily, confident in her own slim beauty and other talents. Completely innocent of course. Jiro would like that. The maid would undoubtedly squeal a bit, but warming the master's bed would do her good. And the mistress, too.

Now that she had begun noticing things, she noticed her own condition. She masturbated faithfully every night, imagining Jiro and sometimes Goemon or Rosamund and, rarely, other lovers she had had in the past. But three weeks of masturbation did her no good. She wondered whether Rosamund would enjoy beating the plump thighs and belly of this maid. Rosamund's own maid, Oko, was a delight and joined their pleasures discreetly whenever necessary. Okiku sighed and licked her lips. Her hands stole to the juncture of her thighs. She would have to do something about the maid, and soon.

A discreet bell tinkled, breaking into her thoughts. Someone had passed through the front gate. A moment later the front door slid back and a high voice called, 'Please forgive me for disturbing you.'

'Otsu, answer the door.'

'Yes, mistress.' The maid rose to her bare feet. She was ungraceful and untutored, Okiku noted, but her plump ass wiggled suggestively as she scurried through the house to the entrance hallway.

'Mistress, it's a nun come to call!' she called out in a high-pitched voice.

Okiku rose swiftly to her feet. At the unpaved entrance hallway stood the muffled figure of a nun. Her hands were hidden in her sleeves, and the candle guttering in the darkening hallway barely showed the shape of her figure. Okiku smiled. There was news, she hoped, from their men.

'Otsu, go to the kitchen and stay there until I call for you. I will attend to the sister. Prepare some of

77

the master's favourite foods. I hope he will be here soon.'

The nun stepped out of her lacquered wooden pattens and stepped up onto the house floor. Okiku embraced her warmly.

'I've been so lonely,' complained the nun. Then the two of them said together, 'Have you heard from –' and burst out laughing. It was clear that loneliness, not news of their missing men, had drawn Rosamund out of the safety of the governor's mansion.

'Come, let us sit in the inner room.' Okiku took her friend by the arm and led her to the room she had been sitting in before. She stirred up the charcoal in the brazier, and they sat down side by side. Feeling the warm softness of her friend brought on a repetition of the lustful thoughts she had been having.

'You've heard nothing?' asked Okiku.

'No,' said Rosamund. 'Those two horny bastards are probably sleeping with every maid in every inn on the Tokaido highway.'

'No, Rosamund – you know how they both are, though I don't deny they probably will have some fun on the way'

'Are you as worried as I?' Rosamund's hand stole into Okiku's.

Okiku tried to put on a brave face. 'No. I don't think they have been arrested, or we would have found out the painful way before now. They are probably working at something, or possibly still waiting for an audience. Also, you must not forget the way takes ten days on foot, and they might have walked rather than taken a ship for some reason.'

'I know,' wailed Rosamund, 'but I'm so horny!' She

turned and kissed Okiku's mouth.

Her soft tongue ran into Okiku like living fire. Okiku half-turned to her and sucked hungrily at the proffered lips. She grasped hungrily at Rosamund's full breasts, and they fell together onto the mat floor.

Rosamund slid her hands down the length of Okiku's slim body. She pressed the darker girl down on the mat and levered herself up on the sweet form. She pulled at the hem of Okiku's robe impatiently and exposed the length of her smooth legs. She twitched the folds of cloth – the robe and the red underskirt – aside and stroked the pads of her fingers up the length of the silky inner thighs.

She touched the moist curls before the juncture of the thighs. Okiku moaned in anticipation and shoved her hips forward to hurry the contact. Rosamund slid her fingertips higher until she could touch the slick lips that hid in the thicket.

Her mouth moved from Okiku's sucking lips to her neck, licking the length of the honey-gold skin. She probed delicately at the entrance to Okiku's cunt, then slid one finger delicately into the dripping channel.

'More, more!' begged the woman beneath Rosamund. A second, then a third digit followed the first. Okiku's hips jerked against the pressure, forcing the fingers deeper and deeper into her body. She pulled the black nun's robe aside and felt the erect nipples that lay above her. She held each large, soft breast in her fist and squeezed. At first she used little pressure; then, in a sudden motion, she clenched each fist, bringing a moan of pleasure and grateful gratification from her friend. She pulled the breasts to her own and frenziedly rubbed Rosamund's

79

nipples against her own erect dark ones.

Rosamund kissed Okiku on the mouth again, probing the depths of that pulling delight with her tongue. She felt Okiku remove her hands from her breasts, and assisted her in stripping off her robe. Suddenly Okiku seemed possessed of demonic energy. She hurled the larger woman off her and rolled her over on her back. She rose to her knees a minute to contemplate the sight that greeted her eyes. Rosamund lay on her back on the floor, legs spread in the candlelight.

Sitting on her knees, Okiku revelled in the sight of her friend. Rosamund was tall and well proportioned. Long, tapering legs joined at generous, rounded hips. Her smooth belly, shadowed in the middle by her sunken navel, sloped down to a delicious forest of blonde curls, moistened and slicked now by her own juices. A prominent clitoris stood well out from the thicket, its tip a gentle contrast to the gold of her pussy hair and the white of her skin. On her thigh, half-hidden by the thicket of rich hair, was a lifelike tattoo of a red rose. Her breasts, generous and large, covered her high rib cage. There the white of the mounds contrasted unashamedly with the bold pink of large areolas and the deeper pink of the erect nipples. Rosamund smiled at her friend in anticipation, and they both held their breaths.

With a wordless cry Okiku threw herself onto the supine body of the blonde. She straddled the waiting face and brought her black-haired cunt down on the waiting mouth. Her own mouth covered the waiting cunt below her. Her teeth dug, none too gently, into the soft, fleshy spike between the lips. Rosamund cried out softly, her face obscured by Okiku's thighs

80

and the skirts of her robe. Mindlessly, knowing Rosamund expected it, Okiku rammed her moist pussy into her friend's mouth. She was rewarded by the delightful touch of a soft tongue, probing into her insides.

She rocked on Rosamund's face with abandon. Her own tongue probed the length of the blonde's cunt, dipping occasionally into the channel or slipping the length of the fleshy lips. Rosamund reciprocated and bucked her mouth and busy tongue against Okiku's sweet-smelling pussy. In the meantime their hands were roving over one another's bodies. Okiku roughly squeezed handfuls of soft flesh and was rewarded with moans of gratitude she could feel, rather than hear.

Their movements became more frenzied. Okiku had her thighs spread as far as she could. The little button of her clitoris was being forced into Rosamund's hungry mouth. At the same time she was roughly mouthing the blonde fur and the fleshy, salty-tasting lips below her. She felt her climax approach. Her strong fingers contracted on the blonde girl's smooth skin, squeezing handfuls painfully. Rosamund raised her hips as high as she could, trying to force the delightful mouth deep into herself. She exploded together with her friend in a series of delightful waves of pleasure.

They withdrew from one another laughing. Their faces were smeared with one another's juices. They kissed long, and each one tasted herself on the other's lips. The kiss continued, and their hands roved over one another's bodies, rekindling the fires that had been only slightly slaked before.

Okiku pushed away her friend and whispered, 'Wait.'

From a lacquered chest of drawers set with black metal finishing she withdrew a box. The box was of some light wood, covered with polished gold lacquer depicting a scene of two mandarin ducks. She placed the box between them and opened it, a mischievous look in her eyes. The box was divided into compartments of various sizes. There were several silvery balls Rosamund did not recognise and some implements of horn, wood, and ivory. Two objects she did recognise, and she smiled at Okiku impishly as the darker woman, her hair hanging down over her face, withdrew one of them.

'This is called a "harigata." Many women use them, particularly in the houses of those with many wives. I'm surprised you haven't seen one before.'

Rosamund laughed. 'Goemon doesn't need them. His women are quite satisfied and well served. I see to that. But this is very pretty.' She fingered the length of the ivory shaft. 'It's smaller than Jiro's.' They laughed together at the shared revelation.

Okiku handed Rosamund the harigata and, giggling, helped her put it on.

'You use it when he gets too tired,' said the blonde girl.

'Jiro is never too tired,' Okiku laughed, her face flushed. 'No, I have him use it when I want more than one hole stuffed.'

'You could always borrow Goemon for a while – provided, of course, you reciprocate.'

'Don't I always?' Okiku giggled, and posed Rosamund so that the ivory staff stood out from her hips like a man's erect prick. Standing, they kissed deeply. Then Okiku sank to the floor seductively. She licked the cuntlips below the harigata for a moment, and Rosamund, her hands on her hips, looked down at her friend over the hills of her own breasts.

Okiku turned away, then knelt with her ass in the air, her neck twisted to see the effect of her position on her friend. Rosamund raised a foot and pushed her big toe into the moist, gaping cunt. The toe slid in for a bit, and Okiku wriggled her ass. The rimming black hairs seemed to beckon the standing woman. Rosamund dropped to her knees behind Okiku. She bent forward and inhaled the delicate musk of her friend's body. Her tongue licked out and traversed the length of the crack between Okiku's buns, lingered for a while at the clenched asshole, then travelled downward to the sopping hole that awaited her.

'Put it in!' urged Okiku.

Rosamund rose to her knees. Guiding her surrogate prick with her hands, she placed it at the waiting entrance. Then she pushed forward, keeping her weight on her knees to spare her friend.

'Lie on top of me!' Okiku demanded furiously. 'Be a man!'

The words galvanised Rosamund. She pushed herself forward, letting her weight crush the slighter woman beneath her. Okiku, used to the far greater weight of her man, minded not at all. She grunted in pleasure as the ivory prick widened her hungry channel. She wiggled her ass backward to force more of the delicious morsel into her burning cleft. She felt the weight and pressure of the two full mounds that depended from her friend's chest. Rosamund moved as if in trance, faster and faster, enjoying in her imagination being a man. Lost in her fantasy, she muttered, 'I'm fucking you, my lovely! Your insides, I'm inside your cunt. You can't get away!... Oh, I'll force you ... More!... More!'

Okiku grinned at hearing her friend's mutterings, which were interspersed with the feel of tongue, lips, and teeth as they licked, sucked, and bit at her neck and back.

'Squeeze my breasts!'

Rosamund complied gently.

'Harder!' ordered Okiku, and Rosamund, her full weight on Okiku's bent back, forced her fingers deep into the firm mounds of flesh.

Moving carefully, so as not to dislodge her friend, Okiku reached a hand for the box and extracted the second harigata. Moving her hands between both their legs, she rammed the other fake prick home. For a moment she thought Rosamund would stop, but soon her friend adjusted happily to the presence of the harigata up her hungry orifice.

Leaning on her elbows, her hands behind her, Okiku frigged her friend. Her motions were slow and controlled at first, but Rosamund's questing fingers and wet mouth titillated her skin, her own movements became rough and fast. The ivory shaft slid in and out of Rosamund's lubricated insides. Every push brought on a responding squeeze from Rosamund, and Okiku shook in doubled response. Their movements became quicker and less controlled. Okiku forced the shaft to its limit up Rosamund, and the blonde girl over her responded roughly as well, driving her tongue into Okiku's ears, biting her shoulders roughly, and squeezing her breasts.

Okiku closed her eyes and tried to imagine that the body rocking on top of her was that of a man – specifically, her own man. The image was shattered by the press of full breasts on her back. Though she

84

enjoyed the sensation of those warm orbs pressing into her, she was conscious that they also spoiled her illusion of masculinity. But the pleasure of being fucked by another person, one she truly loved, soon overcame her again. She moaned with anticipation and twisted her head around to kiss her friend as the waves of her climax started curling inside her. Her lips parted involuntarily, and her mouth was soon filled with Rosamund's delicious tongue. She sucked at the proffered member, licking it over with her own oral digit. At the same time she rammed the harigata into her friend with as much strength as the awkward position allowed.

Rosamund was the first to come. She uttered a moan in the depths of her throat, and her tongue fluttered rapidly against Okiku's. Her hips twisted convulsively, and shudders of pleasure overcame her. Okiku noted the movements, and her own insides melted in concert with her friend. They collapsed together in a pile of gold, black, and white and lay breathing heavily on the floor. Okiku twisted around in her friend's arms and gently extracted the harigata from Rosamund's cunt. She held it out before them, and both admired the slick length; then she brought it to her mouth and ran her tongue along the length. Rosamund giggled appreciatively and kissed her long and deeply.

After they recovered their breath, Okiku poured tea, and the two chatted about minor things. Inevitably, their talk drifted to their men and their absence. Okiku smiled.

'Why the grin, Okiku?'

'It's nothing'

The blonde took Okiku's hand in hers and raised it to her lips. She set her teeth into the palm and closed her jaws none too gently. 'I'll bite if you don't tell me!'

Okiku smacked her friend's cheek lightly. She knew that Rosamund preferred her sex with some violence and was always ready to indulge her.

'I was just thinking that what you just had is not sufficient for you'

Rosamund sighed. 'That's true enough. Much as I love you, if I don't get a man soon, I'll burst – or look for someone outside'

A scuffling sound drew ther attention. Rosamund reached reflexively for her disguising hood.

'It's only the new maid,' said Okiku. 'She's fresh from the country and rather foolish. Quite pretty in a countrified sort of way. I wonder how Jiro will react to her presence. I'll probably have to supervise that...' Her voice drifted off as a thought suddenly occurred to her.

'Rosamund, why should we keep it for Jiro? Why don't you do the office? I'm sure you can, and it will be a new experience for you...'

Rosamund did not follow Okiku's thoughts immediately.

'What office? What are you talking about, Okiku?'

Okiku grinned. 'She's a virgin. She should be made ready for the master of the house, but he's not here'

Rosamund laughed. 'And you expect me to do that?'

'Well, normally the woman of the household should be responsible for inducting a new member, and since you're a member of this household...'

A light of curiosity shone in Rosamund's eyes. Her face turned to the harigata box. 'It sounds like fun...'

'Exactly,' said her friend.

Rosamund looked at herself in a small mirror Okiku provided. A masculine cock stood out from the golden hairs of her cunt. She shivered in pride and pleasure as the maid was called.

Okiku was firm and matter-of-fact, and the maid was too frightened of her mistress and her mistress's guest to make any protest.

'Otsu, the master will be back soon. I am sure he will be wanting you for his pleasure, but I don't want him fatigued by teaching you your business. Our guest has kindly agreed to take your education on herself.'

The maid bowed, half-grateful, half-fearful of what was to come.

'Lie down!' commanded her mistress.

The maid hastily rolled onto her back. Four hands spread her thighs, and then a candle was brought to brighten the scene of the action. For a long moment, Rosamund admired the virgin pussy beneath her. At the bottom of the firm belly a tiny trace of charcoal black blossomed forth into a slick black moss. The faint outline of the virgin slit was visible where the hairs joined along its length. The lips were small and hidden in the soft thicket.

Rosamund's hand gently stroked down the length of the slit, then parted the lips and examined the tiny hole. Her fingers pressed against the membrane that blocked the treasure house for the time being, then withdrew. She knelt between the chunky legs and kissed the virgin slit for a long moment. Her tongue laved the length, paying particular attention to the tiny pearl of the clitoris and the entrance itself. The girl's eyes, which had been staring wildly in fearful anticipation, relaxed and closed to tiny

A faint half smile appeared on her lips.

When the entrance was sufficiently moistened, Rosamund withdrew her head. She knelt between the outflung, quivering legs for a moment. With one hand she adjusted the ivory length. The other parted the now willing lips before her. Otsu held her breath in anticipation.

With a wild cry, Rosamund launched herself onto the maid. The prelubricated shaft rammed into the virgin channel, ripping the fragile hymen at one stretch. Rosamund's weight smacked down on the maid's body, muffling the latter's shriek. Immediately, Rosamund started pumping into the maid with all her strength.

There was a slight sound in the entranceway. Okiku was too involved in the scene before her to notice the giant shadow that crossed the room in a silent bound. A large hand seized her neck, and a second clamped on her mouth.

'Now, what's this?' breathed a voice in her ear.

She twisted around, about to strike out, when the familiar feel of the hands and the strong body stopped her motion. Her tongue slipped out of her lips, and she licked the imprisoning palm. It was relaxed, and she whispered fiercely, 'Oh, you! I'm so glad to see you!'

She twisted around in Jiro's arms for a deep kiss, but his eyes and attention were riveted on the squirming bodies of Rosamund and Otsu on the floor before them.

'If you promise you will take me directly after, I think you could join them.'

'I always have enough,' he whispered back, stripping hastily.

Otsu's gasps of pain were giving way to sounds of

incipient pleasure. Rosamund kissed her eyelids, her nose, her pursed rosebud lips. Suddenly she felt two hands clamp on her full buns. The crack of her ass was parted. A warm, fleshy knob touched the entrance to her cunt. She increased the rapidity of her movements into the maid's quaking body, and just then an enormously long and thick prick pushed into her. Surprised, she squeaked and tried to turn, but Jiro's enormous hands kept her in place. He matched the rhythm of his thrusts to hers. Each time the ivory cock penetrated the maid, the thick flesh shaft penetrated her. His hairy ball bag swung under her, and to Okiku, who crouched before the threesome to enjoy the view, it looked as if Rosamund had suddenly grown male appendages.

Their movements grew quicker and more frenzied, and the maid, overcome by the power of the thrusts, raised two plump legs and tried to throw them over Rosamund's ass. Only when her heels hit Jiro's heaving sides did she realise that she was being mounted by two people, not one. She squealed, whether in terror or in delight, even she could not tell.

All three climaxed together, the maid for the first time in her life with an object in her treasure house. Her moisture came down like rain, wetting her hairs and Rosamund's into a black-and-gold mat. Jiro tensed and pushed his hips as far into Rosamund as he could. His sword jerked two or three times and then gushed forth a jet of liquid that inundated Rosamund's thirsty insides and spilled out in a trickle, further wetting the juncture of her body and the maid's. Overcome, Okiku shoved a hand between the three bodies and was rewarded with Rosamund's heaving twist as she, too, came at the

89

added titillation. When Okiku withdrew her hand, it streamed a thick liquid stream that spattered the matting.

Jiro and Rosamund rolled off the maid, and she lay there, exposed and plump, barely breathing, her eyes closed and her lightly clenched hand covering her rosebud mouth.

Okiku nudged her man with a dainty foot. 'Lazy good-for-nothing, you haven't finished.'

Jiro held onto Okiku's foot and pulled her to him. He bit her calf gently for a moment and looked straight up to her moist, moss-covered cleft. The long, plump slit winked at him from between its thicket as if challenging him to continue. His prick responded to that familiar invitation with a series of twitches that almost immediately brought it to the ready.

Okiku snorted disdainfully. 'No, not yet. There is work before play.' She knelt by the maid and raised her to a sitting position. 'The master is home. You must greet him properly!'

The dazed maid, who until now had been half-aware that the master of the house was present, gathered her wits. She bowed immediately and called out in a high-pitched voice the traditional greeting, 'Welcome home!'

Okiku held her by the nape of the neck. 'The master will require his bath, and you, you lazy creature, have not prepared it.' Before the befuddled maid could respond, her mistress continued. 'No matter. You will wash him now. We can prepare a full bath later.'

She motioned Jiro to stand, then had the maid kneel before him in the formal position, knees tucked under her, trunk erect. Then she pulled at

Jiro's hardening prick and placed it at the girl's mouth. 'Wash him properly,' she commanded, and squatted by Rosamund's side to watch.

At first Otsu could not come to grips with the situation. The enormous prick, much thicker than her wrist, would not bend sufficiently for her to reach it from her kneeling position. She licked the heavy bag beneath the shaft, gently caressing the two heavy balls inside. Then she licked the length of the shaft as far as she could reach. The more she licked, the firmer the shaft became and the more difficult it was for her to get closer to the tip.

At last, at a command from Okiku, who with Rosamund could barely restrain her laughter, she grasped the shaft firmly and bent it to her mouth. Now she was able to lick and clean the plum-shaped head, screwing her tongue into the tiny eye at the tip. Jiro's prick was bent uncomfortably at an angle to the vertical, when its natural inclination was to rise to the heavens. Jiro tried to protest but was hushed by his women.

'Samurai do not resist pain!' Okiku said fiercely. 'Now put it into your mouth,' she commanded the girl.

With great effort, Otsu managed to open her mouth wide enough to accommodate the tip of the shaft. Her small, rounded rosebud mouth was distended by the monster prick, which was now rimmed by the red line of her lips. He forced the prick slightly forward, but she gagged and tried to retreat. Taking pity on her, Jiro removed his member from her gaping mouth, and she swallowed convulsively.

'You have much to learn, girl,' said Okiku. Without pause, she rose to her knees, grasped the erect member, and sucked it into her mouth. Jiro moved back and forth lightly, enjoying the warm sensation he had missed for so long. She tickled the tip of his prick for a moment, then withdrew. Rosamund promptly took her place, while Otsu looked on in fascination. The head disappeared again, apparently without any effort, in the blonde's mouth.

Jiro, knowing Rosamund's preferences, was rougher this time, shoving forward with strong, deep movements. Okiku stopped him with a gesture, then told the maid to bow again. She moved Jiro behind the maid and spread the girl's plump buttocks. Jiro was charmed by the sight. She had a dimple on the side of each buttock, and in between, the tiny bud of her rear entrance beckoned intriguingly. He knelt behind the shivering girl.

Seeing his target, Okiku stopped him and redirected his lance to the softer, wetter cunt. 'No, Jiro,' she said. 'We will leave that one for later. After all, we must leave some entertainment for other times. She has been pierced but has never felt a man. Show her.'

The penetration this time was pleasanter than when Rosamund had taken her virginity, but the thickness of Jiro's prick was such that Otsu could not restrain a scream. The giant prick came up her with a rush, widening and further stretching the tissue that had been so bruised by Rosamund's treatment. The monster prick rested for a while in the channel of her cunt, soaking in the oily, pungent liquids of her femininity.

She inched forward slightly, to ease her position; then her body reasserted itself, and she drove herself backward, impaling herself deeply on the waiting prick. Jiro withdrew, then pushed himself forward once again. She egged him on, moving her body, reluctant to lose the full morsel of engorged flesh that filled an aching cavity she had not known she had. Their movements became more and more rapid, and the pain of penetration receded into memory.

Small grunts and cries came from her mouth. She fell forward and fondled her own tits, pinching the nipples and squeezing them until several hands came to help her. Another hand set to work sliding smoothly along the lips of her cunt as they clutched and sucked at the rapidly moving prick. At last the tension became too strong to bear. Her cries and grunts of ecstasy mingled in a long, uninterrupted wail.

As if feeling the coming climax, the prick that pierced her increased its movements to a blur, a sawing motion that seemed destined never to stop. Her insides clenched, and her whole body shook as wave after wave shook her frame. From the rampant pole she felt an unfamiliar sensation. It quivered and seemed to glow and grow in her belly. Then powerful streams spattered her insides as she let down a little torrent of moisture. Her strength deserted her, and she remained hanging by her cunt from her master's prick, whose pulsing rapidly subsided.

Okiku pulled Jiro's massive frame from the girl. Roughly she jerked his flaccid prick once, then again. The rod, not without effort, remembered its duties. She forced Jiro to a seat on two seating pads, then spitted herself carefully on his manhood, erect once again. Her ass nestled comfortably on his hairy thighs.

93

'Come here,' she commanded the maid, who had barely recovered from her climax. Okiku pushed the girl's face down to her open crotch. As Okiku rode up and down the fleshy column she had the maid lick the length of the shaft and her own gaping cunt. Excited by the sights she had seen and directed, she quickly reached a screaming climax herself. Her inner muscles squeezed repeatedly at Jiro's shaft, but she came alone in single splendour, ramming Otsu's face roughly into her mound as she reached the peak.

Okiku rose from Jiro's rapidly deflating prick, and he lay back gratefully on the floor. 'I've just walked from Osaka, a full day's walk, and now I really must have a bath. But it was a wonderful welcome.'

'You see, Rosamund?' said Okiku sweetly. 'He doesn't get tired, so I keep the harigata only to add to my pleasure, not to replace him.'

Rosamund laughed. 'Dear Okiku, I never doubted him one bit. But where's Goemon?' she asked Jiro.

He muttered something incomprehensible, and both women pummelled him until he raised his head. 'He stayed in Osaka. He had some business to attend to. Let me have a short nap and a bath, and I'll tell you everything over supper.'

During the meal, a plain one of grilled salt fish and udon noodles, Jiro told them the tale, including the clues they had managed to unearth.

Rosamund was puzzled. 'Why doesn't the shogun just arrest those responsible and hang them?'

Jiro turned to her and sighed. He was too tired for a lengthy political lecture, the details of which were hazy to him as well.

'I'll try to explain. The shogun is not an absolute ruler. He is the most powerful baron, with the full support of his clan, the Tokugawa, and of related clans such as the Matsudaira clans.'

'That's Goemon's family name,' Rosamund pointed out.

'Yes, and the name of several other families and fiefs, all of whom are junior branches or descendants of Tokugawa retainers. Not all of them are equally loyal. In addition, there are allied barons, who sided with the Tokugawa at the battle of Sekigahara, and opponent barons and clans, who opposed him there and at Osaka. Any of those might wish to depose the supremacy of the Tokugawa clan. To add to that, the shogun rules by a mandate from the emperor.' He had to use the English word here. 'The emperor resides here in Miyako, and one of Goemon's major official duties is to keep an eye on him, or rather on anyone who might use the All under Heaven to try to get support for a rebellion.

'If one of the chief rebels is someone supposedly loyal to the Tokugawa, and he is publicly exposed, there will be muttering, and possibly other people will get the idea that the Tokugawa camp is in disarray. We must stop that at all costs.'

'What are you going to do, then?' asked Rosamund.

'*We*,' said Okiku, succinctly and firmly. Jiro knew better than to try to persuade her. She was a formidable fighter in her own right, a trained assassin and an expert spy. Her family had been ninja in the Kaga mountains for generations.

'Yes, we. It is very simple. We will identify the members of the plot and kill them.'

'From what you said of the kuge who is involved, we will have to enter the court quarter to identify him. The kuge rarely leave their quarter and the palace, you know,' Okiku said thoughtfully. 'I will have to do that. You, my love, are too conspicuous.'

Jiro nodded in agreement as Rosamund asked, 'What are kuge?'

'The noblemen and retainers of the All under Heaven. Their movements are restricted to keep them out of mischief. They are highly inbred, the most refined people in the world, and keep very much to themselves.'

Rosamund, who had lived a very restricted life in many ways since coming to the Japans, looked puzzled. She could not conceive of a group of noblemen restricted in any way by their inferiors. In England, where she was born, and the Lowlands and Spain, where she had grown up, noblemen made their own rules. This new bit of information was something to add to the store of startling information about her adopted country that she already possessed but only half-understood.

The alarm bell tinkled quietly. The three tensed for a moment, wondering who would disturb them at this time. Okiku hurried to the door in time to hear a tentative hurried scratching and a feminine voice call, 'Forgive me for disturbing you.'

She unbarred the door cautiously, Jiro standing by, his massive frame a guarantee against a trap. The small postern door, which forced a visitor to bow in order to enter, opened a crack, and Oko, Rosamund's slim maid, slipped through.

'Is my master here?' she asked, while still rising from her bow. Her tone was anxious.

'No,' said Jiro kindly. 'He will return in a few days. Your mistress is here, though.'

The slim girl bit her lip and almost wrung her hands in her anxiety. Okiku urged her up into the house, and she shed her wooden pattens and climbed onto the raised tatami mat. Notwithstanding her agitation, Jiro had time to admire her slim feet as she hurriedly knelt and tucked them under her.

She produced from the folds of her robe an envelope addressed, 'Goemon, a doctor, by hand of my daughter Oko.'

'This is by my former mistress. She is now a nun in a nunnery called Dosojin-ji, not far from the town of Yoshida . . .'

She stopped at the cries of surprise that came from both Okiku and Jiro. Okiku was laughing. She had been in Dosojin-ji for some days, and the interesting customs of the nuns had taught her much. Jiro remembered the town of Yoshida with less favour. While Okiku had been enjoying the hospitality of the nunnery, he had been prisoner of the murderous lord of the town, Matsudaira Nobutaka.

Oko continued: 'This is not her usual style of writing. She is greatly disturbed, I can tell. I am sure my master would be able to help her, whatever the trouble.'

Jiro reached for the letter. She hesitated for a moment, then, recalling that the samurai before her was a blood brother of her own master and that both had enjoyed her together on many an occasion, she surrendered the letter.

Jiro opened the sheet and read it out loud.

'To Goemon the itinerant doctor, and something else. In this, the period of the iris bloom, I write to ask your assistance. We in the nunnery of Dosojin-

97

ji have been plagued by evil men. We have no one to turn to. The blow fell from above. If you are able, I would beg your assistance. At Dosojin-ji.'

'She is afraid to put too much onto paper, for fear it will be intercepted,' hazarded Jiro.

'Someone must go there at once,' said Oko with unusual heat. They knew from experience that she was a restrained girl who suppressed all expressions of emotion, even at critical moments.

'You had better go, Okiku said to Jiro.

'But Goemon will be expecting me here when he arrives!'

'At the moment we have no information anyway. Go and see what is happening, then return here. It is a matter of honour for both Goemon and myself. If you don't go, I will have to. Besides' – her eyes gleamed for a moment – 'a visit to a religious establishment will do you good.' Particularly that establishment, she thought to herself. She had never been too explicit about her experiences in Dosojin-ji, preferring to let their teachings be a constant surprise and delight to her companions.

'I'll leave tomorrow,' said Jiro, still not fully convinced. 'Maybe Goemon will have arrived by then.'

Okiku kissed him thankfully, and Oko bowed her gratitude, repeating over and over, 'Oh, thank you, thank you.'

Chapter 6

Dark night covered the city of Miyako. Climbing lightly over blank walls and running silently over the tiled roof ridges, Okiku made her way through the city. She wore rough brown-stained clothes that did not limit her movements and blended in easily with the dark woodwork of the houses. Her straw sandals absorbed all sound, and even the straight sword strapped to her shoulders was wrapped so as not to make a betraying sound. A dark cloth wrapped her face and head, leaving only a slit for her eyes.

She had spent several days trying to track down the kuge, following the hints supplied by Jiro. For two nights now she had been stalking the rooftops, checking and eliminating possibilities. She crouched over a branch that overlooked a darkened villa. Below her was the delicate tracery of a formal garden. Artful rocks, well trimmed azalea bushes, a small bamboo grove, and the elderly twisted pine on whose branches she was crouching complemented the straight lines of the villa's verandah. The garden reflected in the still waters of a small pond, and Okiku considered her next move. From a neighbouring house, where some sort of social event was in progress, she could hear the murmur of talk and occasional bursts of laughter. The sounds would cover any noise she made during entry.

She leaped from her branch to a rock and from there, with hardly more sound than the wind, to the verandah, where she landed silently and crouched, listening. There was no response from inside the villa. She took a special tool from a hidden pouch and silently pried out one of the wooden shutters that closed the villa in for the night. The heavy board slid out from its tracks easily. She moved it aside and crouched, ear to the floorboards, listening again.

Slipping inside past a sliding paper-glazed door, she found herself in a tatami-floored room. The room showed great elegance – the metal fittings on the sliding doors were beautifully worked, and under her fingers Okiku could feel embroidered borderings on the tatami mats. But the elegance was not supported by wealth. The mats had not been replaced for many years, and there were scuffed spots in mats and borders. One of the fusuma sliding doors had been torn and never mended or replaced, and over all there was a musty smell.

She inched carefully forward and slid into another room. This one had been recently occupied, but there was nothing there to excite her interest. She ventured out into the wooden-floored corridor that ran along both rooms. She cautiously tested the first step. There were no traps or alarms. More boldly, she slithered across the hall to the closed room on the other side.

Her sensitive foot suddenly noted a change as one of the floorboards sank beneath her. Using her other foot, she pushed herself into the air just as the board made a squeaking sound. This was a nightingale floor, which announced the presence of an intruder. As she leaped, her head brushed a cobweb. She clawed for a hold on the beam that served as a lintel over the entry to the rooms, and suddenly found herself entangled in a mesh of silken ropes that fell from above. In the depths of the house, she could hear a series of musical notes announcing her arrival.

She struggled to release herself from the enveloping cords but soon had to desist. They were made of raw silk, slick and tough, and small, sharp hooks were embedded in the mesh, hampering every movement and sticking deep into her flesh whenever she moved. Before she could think of a more successful method of extricating herself, a door at the far end of the corridor slid open, and she was illuminated by the light of a single lampion.

'Well, what have we here?' said a cultured voice in an amused tone. 'A little mouse, struggling to get free.'

She redoubled her efforts, sliding a hand to her waist, where she carried a small razor.

'No, no. We mustn't,' said the figure. As the man slid forward, Okiku could see that he wore the tall hat and baggy trousers of a kuge. The curved blade of an antique sabre glinted in the light of the candle as the kuge positioned it at Okiku's throat. The kuge's tone was high and unnatural, as if he were a No actor playing a part. She could not see his face, but she felt that his lips must be curled in an

101

expression of amusement.

'What? Nothing to say? How gauche. We must find out what you are doing here. So messy, too. And just when I'm due at a most interesting party.'

From among the folds of his robe he produced several lengths of silk cord. Cautiously and with much effort he bound the struggling Okiku. When she was fully bound he hauled her into one of the tatami rooms and laid her on the floor against a pillar. He removed the hooked cords of his trap, then attached her to the pillar. From a capacious sleeve he produced a long scarf. Without warning or change of expression, he punched her in her middle. She *oofed* in surprise, and he shoved the wadded scarf into her mouth.

'Well, that will keep you from suicide until I'm ready to ask questions. I couldn't possibly miss the party of Lord Sakaue, the minister of the right.'

He set himself back to admire his handiwork. This was the first time Okiku had ever had to examine a kuge openly. He had a long, regular face with a hooked nose. His eyebrows were arched, and his face had been made up with white powder and rouge cheeks and lips. His hair was brushed back from a high forehead into the tall black gauze hat he wore.

'I am afraid I shall have to leave you now. Some of my servants will come and keep guard over you. Call out as much as you will – people are used to loud calls from this mansion.'

Okiku squirmed angrily, but he had displayed a knowledge of knots and ties that was usually the forte of constable samurai. Her hands were tied behind her in an intricate yoke that connected wrists, elbows, and neck and attached her to a strong house post.

The tall kuge rose unhurriedly and smiled down at his captive. Then he left the room through one of the sliding doors that connected to another series of rooms. Okiku was left alone with her thoughts, still struggling to loosen her bonds.

The door to the corridor slid aside, and a young man was bowing at the entrance. 'Excuse me for interrupting you. The Lady Gojo-no-Satsuki is attending you. She is on her way to –' The young man, a servant by his dress, stopped, mouth open at the sight of the bound figure before him. He seemed incapable of speech for a long moment.

'Mizuno-no-kami-sama,' a new, high pitched female voice called out. From behind the kneeling servant, Okiku saw the figure of a stately woman peering into the room. Her hair hung down her back, caught by a single ribbon. Her face was pale and of an almost perfect oval shape. A high forehead rose smoothly to the hairline. Her eyebrows had been shaved off, and two smudges had been painted high up on her forehead instead, giving her face with its rosebud mouth a look of perpetual surprise. Looking carefully, wondering what the new figure portended for her future, Okiku had time to note the shrewdness of the eyes in the masklike face.

'Who are you?' Gojo-no-Satsuki demanded. 'Matsuo, release the gag and mask.'

The servant did so. When he approached, Okiku could see that he was a handsome young lad, in his mid-teens. He drew a sharp breath once her mask was off.

'It's a woman!'

'What!' said the lady. She swept forward to examine the captive. 'Who are you?' she demanded.

Okiku bowed in her bonds.

'I came here by mistake. I wish no one any harm.'

'You are a ninja? Or just a plain common thief?'

She noted Okiku's smooth face and makeup. 'No, you could not be a thief. Your face is not coarse enough. I am an expert at physiognomy. What are you doing here?'

Okiku stirred nervously. 'He will be back soon,' she warned.

Appearing to make up her mind suddenly, Gojo-no-Satsuki said decisively, 'Listen to me carefully. I will help you get out of here. I see you are not a thief. But I have need of one such as you from the outside. Would you like a bargain? Quick – Mizuno-no-kami is returning with his servants.'

'Yes,' said Okiku succinctly, hoping against hope.

The other woman nodded. 'I will release and hide you. You will do something for me, something private. To ensure you do so, I will also promise a reward on completion. Do we agree?'

'Yes,' said Okiku. She knew this would be the only chance offered.

The lady knelt by Okiku's side. A sharp poignard emerged from the mass of tresses that fell down her back.

'Matsuo, take her and hide her in Lord Sakaue's tea-house. It will not be used tonight. Climb over the wall. I will see you there.' She smiled warmly at the young serving lad. He blushed, and ducked his head as she stroked his shoulder.

'Yes – yes, mistress. I will do it all.'

'I will be *most* grateful...' The last word lingered on her lips as she rose to go.

Dragging Okiku, the young servant crept out of the mansion, while Gojo-no-Satsuki went back to the waiting room. When the master of the house returned with his armed servants, Okiku was nowhere to be seen. Lay Gojo-no-Satsuki was waiting demurely in the anteroom of the mansion, her two maids in attendance.

'Ah, Lady Gojo-no-Satsuki, so kind of you to wait for my worthless self. I fear I must delay you for yet a while. A thief has broken into the mansion, and I must have my servants search him out.'

Lady Gojo-no-Satsuki covered her mouth with her fan. 'How frightening. I shall await you here, then. It will undoubtedly be too unsafe to venture out.'

He bowed to her hastily, and she could hear him ordering his servants to arm themselves and search the premises and the neighbourhood. Idly, she wondered why the escape of one thief, or possibly ninja spy, could excite such activity. As they left Mizuno-no-kami's mansion, armed servants spread out through the garden and the neighbouring streets to search for the former captive.

Okiku sat in the tiny teahouse massaging her limbs. The servant knelt beside her in the dark, his breath whispering in her ear. Outside she could hear the noises of the party in another wing of the villa. At last the low door – too small to walk through; one had to crawl – slid open. Okiku tensed, but she was calmed by a familiar flowery smell she had noticed before.

'We must talk quickly,' whipered her rescuer. 'Mizuno-no-kami must be desperate. His servants are searching the mansions around and will soon be here. He concocted some excuse. You must be hidden. I have a very good place, but is your hair long?'

Surprised at the question, Okiku muttered a low-pitched affirmative.

'I will hide you among the partygoers. The guessing game is about to start, and it will take an hour or more. By the time it is over, Mizuno-no-kami's men will have finished searching and you will be able to escape. You must promise that after you escape, you will come to see me again. You can easily find the place.' There was a hint of desperation in the last sentence.

Again, Okiku gave her assent, not knowing fully what she was assenting to.

'Put these on!' ordered Gojo-no-Satsuki, and passed Okiku a rich brocade robe. 'Don't worry about tying it properly. The game is about to start, and it will not matter anyway. Whatever you do, make no sound and little movement. When it is made dark again, I will get you to an outer door, Matsuo, take her clothes.'

Okiku wanted to ask many questions but was hushed with a quick 'Hurry – there's no time!' Matsuo the servant disappeared with her clothes and equipment, and Gojo-no-Satsuki led her towards the sounds of gaiety and laughter.

The lamps were being extinguished as she was led into a room of silent smiling women, all dressed in rich multi-layered gowns, all made up as Gojo-no-Satsuki was. Their makeup glimmered in the gloom. There was much muffled giggling as the twenty-odd women sorted themselves into a line. Then, to Okiku's surprise, they opened their robes, lifting the skirts behind them. An attendant hurriedly passed down the row and arranged each robe to frame its owner in layers of bright colours as they sank down to sit formally on their knees, though the knees were much farther apart than etiquette would normally have allowed. Okiku, still dazed by her escape and her surroundings, followed suit. Two female attendants hurriedly arranged a hanging curtain across the room. The curtain hid the faces and bodies of the women completely but ended at the level of their navels. Their knees projected beyond, and the row of furry grottoes was exposed to whoever would bend down to view it under the curtain.

'Are you ready?' a male voice called from outside the room.

'A moment!' called out one of the women. The rest giggled as she added in a whisper, 'That will make them more anxious.'

She called out again, and the sliding door opened, to admit a row of men, all blindfolded. They were led by an older, plumper man, whose uncovered eyes glinted with mirth. The men's side of the room was better lit with candles, and by pressing her face to the curtain, Okiku could faintly see their figures through the layers of coloured gauze that made up the curtain. The other women peeked through the curtain in a similar way.

'Furukawa-no-Tadauchi-sama has bet he will get all twenty right. Others have bet on smaller numbers,' announced the older man with satisfaction. The men all held flat shaku sceptres in their hands, and they nudged one another expectantly.

The sliding doors to the garden were removed, and a cool breeze blew from the garden into the room. Okiku could barely suppress an urge to rise and escape. It was the half-caught glimpse of armed servants in large numbers searching the garden that restrained her.

The fat man, whom others addressed as Sakauesama, obviously the host, called out a name. The first kuge knelt before the first woman in line. He bowed, and she bowed in return. She spread her knees wider and leaned back. He brought his face between her legs and took a deep breath, then crept backward, bowed again, and murmured a polite, 'Thank you.' A fan-folded sheet of paper lay on the shaku. With deft movements the man wrote a line, then moved to the next kneeling woman. Again he bowed, sniffed carefully, and at length retreated, bowed, and wrote on the folded strip, now open to a clean rib, the shaku serving to support the paper.

When the first man reached his fifth trial, Sakaue sent another man to the start. The first man, apparently the boastful Furukawa-no-Tadauchi, seemed hesitant at the eighth try. After sniffing ecstatically for a long moment, he retreated a bit, bowed again, and announced, 'I must make a second test.'

Sakaue admonished him delightedly. 'You will lose points Furukawa-sama!'

'The scent of the peaches was a delight to Goku, but even he must taste the fruit to reach immortality.'

The Chinese quotation so delighted the audience that they laughed heartily, and Sakaue waved a hospitable hand. 'Please help yourself, Furukawa-sama.'

Furukawa bent forward with a murmured 'Forgive my disturbing you' and ran his tongue up the length of the pouting slit before him. The lady behind the curtain barely twitched, but Okiku, who was not far from her, could see that her head lolled back in pleasure.

The game continued. The men sniffed the ladies'

108

scents and, when puzzled, used the more accurate taste test, losing points in consequence. At the first sniff of the black-gauze-covered head, Okiku was terrified. Gojo-no-Satsuki, who was beside her, smiled and motioned for calm with her hand. At the second man, Okiku was relaxed enough to enjoy the thought of a man's sniffing at her entrance without a taste of the delights inside. Her own men, she knew, would not have resisted the temptation. As more men passed her, and an occasional one tasted the delights of her pursed nether lips, her juices began to run with greater freedom, and she became caught up in the delight of the game. Fantastic images rose into her mind, and she had to restrain her hands from dipping into her own flesh.

A whispered, laughing disagreement distracted her. One of the men could not make up his mind. The tongue test had apparently proved inconclusive. A second test was debated and eventually assented to.

'It will cost you ten full points!' Sakaue warned the gallant.

The man bowed silently. He loosened his trousers, and through the gauze Okiku could catch sight of an erect male member. Easing forward in a squat, the man pressed the tip of his prick into the soft, waiting cranny, as the woman behind the curtain bent backward to facilitate entry. There was not much room to manoeuvre, the position being so awkward, but eventually the man was able to make a decision.

The line moved on. More of the men had recourse to the final test. A man approached Okiku. He was pale skinned and rather thin. He bowed to her ceremoniously, then bowed deeped and sniffed appreciatively at her cunt. He took a second breath, then signalled lazily with his fan. Bowing once again, he applied his lips to Okiku's. She almost gasped at the touch. His thin lips caressed her cunt-lips delicately. His tongue peeped out and stroked her clitoris. Okiku could not tell whether it was the anticipation or the strange surroundings, but she felt her pulse hammer in her ears as her hips jerked at his sucking mouth.

He tongued her inconclusively for a long while, tasting her essences and stimulating her tiny clitoris thoughtfully. At last he withdrew, bowed to her once again, and wrote a name on his guessing sheet.

A second and a third man took his place. Okiku was almost weeping with sexual tension now. She fought hard to restrain herself. Only the impassive faces of the women to either side of her restrained her. Obviously they were either more familiar with the game or more experienced in hiding their feelings.

Another man bowed before her. He too could not identify her from her natural scent alone. He tongued her thoughtfully for a few moments, then withdrew. He signalled with his fan, and the master of ceremonies marked his score sheet.

He bowed to her formally again, then extricated his prick from its covering. It was long and thin, an a tiny clear droplet quivered at its tip. The kuge gave it a gentle stroke, then edged forward between Okiku's knees. The tip of his instrument touched the lips of her cunt. He paused for a moment, savouring the sensation. Then he pushed steadily forward, the entire length of his pole disappearing into Okiku's hungry cunt. She bit her lip to restrain her moan of content, and suddenly the muscles of her cunt contracted in a powerful orgasm. Her nails dug deeply into the flesh of her ass as she restrained herself from movement. The man, obviously knowing what he was doing to her, moved his hips and prick in imperceptible circles as her slippery cunt contracted around him with spasms of pleasure.

He moved out of her, and she recovered her composure. Looking around her in embarrassment, she suddenly realised something that had not been clear to her before. It seemed she was not the only one enjoying the competition. The impassivity of her female companions revealed itself for what it really was: Twitches of skin and fingers betrayed the powerful orgasms that were racking them, as the men gradually gave up their attempts to identify their fair companions and resorted to more directly physical methods.

She came many more times that night!

Dressed in the formal finery of a samurai woman, Okiku walked into the kuge quarter the following morning. She found the mansion that had been described to her, and after knocking discreetly, she was immediately admitted into the presence of her saviour of last night. The two women examined one another for a long moment. Gojo-no-Satsuki was older than she had seemed the previous night, Okiku decided. She must be thirty, at least. Her smooth face, under the thick layer of white rice-flour makeup, gave evidence of considerable beauty. The old-fashioned makeup made her look a bit like an antique doll, an effect enhanced by the multitude of robes she wore.

The kuge lady saw before her a young woman, dressed in quiet, modern elegance. Her hair was built up in a series of buns and elaborate pins, her

111

eyebrows were unshaven, and her face was darker than common in women of rank, evidence of a life spent at least partly in the outdoors. There was no evidence that this elegant young woman was a trained killer and spy, though undoubtedly Gojo-no-Satsuki had sufficient protection about her.

They drank tea facing a tiny garden where moss-covered rocks were shaded by a growing vine. Neither touched on the subject of the previous night.

'It is most tiresome,' said Gojo-no-Satsuki after a pause in their talk.

'Indeed?' said Okiku politely.

'Yes,' said Gojo-no-Satsuki. 'Kuge are confined here to this quarter as prisoners. Parties, excursions to temples, games – I am sick and tired of it. It would be nice to be free. It would be nice to live as one wants, without the restraints of custom – as you do...'

Okiku smiled gently. 'I am bound by custom too.'

Gojo-no-Satsuki shook her head. 'No. Not like the kuge. Here everything we do is regulated by customs a thousand years old. I've been married since I was a child and had lovers by the score, always with the same politeness, always the same tiresome games, always the same foods at the same time...' Her voice rose with passion, and she slapped an exquisite teapot away petulantly. It smashed on the garden rocks.

She turned fiercely to Okiku. 'You must help me. I need to get away from this. My inheritance is held by my husband. It is a deed for land on which rent is owed in the Gion quarter. Get it for me. And also... and also, you must teach me how to live in the world. In the real world, not this... this... illusion.' She

112

wiped a tear dramatically with her sleeve.

Okiku gazed at the garden and thought of what the woman before her had said. She could not imagine the life Gojo-no-Satsuki was describing. Her own had been adventurous and, she had to admit, relatively free of restrictions. She was not eager to involve herself in affairs that were not her own, but Gojo-no-Satsuki had helped her and trusted her, and she saw no way out of the obligation.

'What must I do?'

'My husband you know. He is Mizuno-no-kami, in whose house I found you. The situation of his mansion is familiar to you. In an inner room is a lacquered chest. In it are the various deeds to the property he owns, as well as my own. Secure it for me. I will, in the meantime, make preparations for leaving this place. A suicide, a drowning in the river with a proper poetic note, will be appropriate, I think. Then I can live happily.'

'He will wonder about the Gion property,' warned Okiku.

'Oh, no,' said the kuge lady innocently. 'You will have to steal all the papers. By the time he has recovered them (and we shall return them in time), he will have forgotten its existence.'

Okiku had her doubts about this, but she wanted to enter the mansion again, for her own purposes. A place that well protected would undoubtedly have something hidden. Idly she asked, 'What will you do? Surely the Gion property will not maintain you in the fashion to which you are accustomed.'

Gojo-no-Satsuki looked Okiku in the eye and said, 'I believe I will become a courtesan. After all, it is the only thing I really excel at. The house in Gion will be

113

a good place to start. I understand several places of entertainment are being established there.'

Okiku's mouth opened. 'You will... you will become of very low status, then.'

'But it will be most enjoyable. Tell me, are commoner men as direct as they seem? I see you are married. Surely you can instruct me.'

'My man is not exactly a commoner. He is a ronin, an unattached samurai, second son of a hatamoto of the shogun,' Okiku said, a trifle stiffly.

'A hatamoto? Is that some kind of official?'

Okiku stared in surprise at the words. Everyone knew, she had thought, that the shogun's personal officers were called hatamoto. This last sentence suddenly made clear the isolation of the woman who sat before her. She nodded.

'Anyway,' continued Gojo-no-Satsuki, 'you must tell me about men...'

'They are wonderful. Actually, all men are wonderful in bed, provided they are well managed and, like horses, not ridden too often for too long.'

They laughed together.

'That is why the profession of courtesan is so suited for me. I shall be able to change mounts as I please.'

'You might not be your own mistress,' warned Okiku. 'The life of a courtesan is not easy. Many prey upon her.'

'I have my defences,' said Gojo-no-Satsuki calmly. 'We kuge are helpless before the mass of the samurai, but individually, we have our ways...'

Okiku continued, 'Until and unless you become really successful, you will not be able to choose your lovers freely. Why, you might have to take very simple people – servants, for instance.'

'That would not disturb me. You have no idea how tiresome life has been. I shall be delighted at any change. You will do it? Do say yes, please! In any case, you said you would.'

Okiku nodded. She was still not convinced of the wisdom of her move, but she must investigate the mansion again anyway. The trap had sprung before she had managed to survey the premises.

'I will do it,' she said quietly. 'You must tell me the layout of the mansion. Why do you not live there, with your husband?'

'Live with my husband? What an odd idea. Both his and my life would be so terribly restricted. How could I possibly receive lovers except in my own house? Of course, we lived together after the marriage for a while, but I have had a separate establishment for quite a while now, and of course, he has other wives too. I am ashamed to say I am merely his second, you know.'

Okiku delicately changed the subject. 'Is there a room decorated with an azalea motif in the villa?'

'I have no idea. It is rather large, you see, and I never concerned myself with the inner rooms. Each room is named for a flower, though, so there may be one decorated with azaleas. I will describe the chest I want. I believe it is in his study.' She dimpled. 'I bought the chest for him myself, as a gift, and he promised he would use it. There is a hidden compartment...'

Chapter 7

'Is this the Dosojin-ji temple?' The deep masculine voice made the woman behind the gate cower into herself. She clutched her makeshift bamboo spear tightly, and when she spoke, she tried to control the quaver in her voice.

'Who are you?'

'I am a messenger for a certain Goemon, a doctor...' the voice trailed off.

'What does he look like?' the woman asked, still suspicious.

'Young, powerful build. And a very strong sword.'

The woman relaxed a trifle. She opened the postern gate and stepped back. A huge bulk appeared at the opening, and when the man straightened up, she saw before her a giant samurai, with the hairdo of a ronin. She gasped, nonplussed for a moment. Without a word he handed her a purple kerchief and the letter she had written many days before. She recognised the kerchief as her own, one she had left to Goemon some time before. It had wrapped a gift of a pair of swords.

She bowed. 'I am Suhei, sometime wife of Yanagi Kibei of Kamakura. I sent the letter to Goemon. He is not here?'

The giant samurai bowed. 'Miura Jiro. No, Goemon does not yet know. I am his companion, and I hurried ahead. A message has been sent to him.' He looked thoughtfully around at the broken woodwork, the roughly repaired gate and door. 'What happened here?'

'We were attacked again. Men who are, I think, those of Lord Matsudaira Nobutaka of Yoshida –' she broke off as she noticed the samurai's jaw clench. 'We – we managed to identify one of them . . . They killed the prioress and our gatekeeper and some of the other nuns. They took with them two of our novices, and we have not heard from them again. I am greatly afraid this will happen again. The men who attacked us were very amused, you see. Their master, we heard, intended to return again. We have been fearing their attack any night.'

'You may relax now. I will stay until tomorrow.'

'Until tomorrow? What good will that do us?' Yanagi demanded furiously.

'Tomorrow I will go to the Yoshida mansion and restore the balance. In the meantime, I would appreciate a bath and some food. I have been riding for two days and nights.'

She bowed contritely. 'Of course. I apologise. Please follow me.'

He turned to follow her, but a sound from the road outside the massive wall stopped him. There was a rough banging on the door, which Yanagi had forgotten to bar, and it burst open. Several male figures slipped rapidly through the door. Upon seeing the samurai before them, they drew to a halt. Jiro, who had had some warning, was less taken aback. He drew his great sword as he pivoted, and it cut out in a gleaming horizontal arc at chest height. He twisted his wrist and raised his arm, and the sword was held with two hands above his head. The two foremost of the men seemed to gasp and gurgle. A flood of blood streamed through their throats, which Jiro's quick draw had cut neatly through. As they fell Jiro took a giant step forward, and his sword cut with an audible thunk into the skull of a third of the figures.

Four were left. Their swords whispered from lacquered scabbards, and they manoeuvred for position around the murderous giant who confronted them. He grinned at them and feinted at the nearest, who leaped back. Jiro turned suddenly on the one to his extreme right, exposing his back to the thug on his left. Stepping forward, the man aimed a cut at the broad back. He screamed suddenly as the point of Jiro's short sword, drawn under the cover of his arm and held blade backward, stabbed into his belly. Jiro recovered and faced his three remaining opponents. One of them suddenly screamed, a high-pitched, almost womanly sound. A pointed bamboo pushed out of the soft part of his belly as Yanagi rammed her makeshift spear into his kidney.

The scream was the final straw for the remaining two attackers. They turned to go. It was unfortunate for them that the door they had pushed open not a minute before was a postern door that forced one to bend to get through it. As they attempted to leave, they heard the thin scream of two blades, a short and a long one, cleaving the air before they cleaved the raiders' spines.

Yanagi turned one of the dead men over. Her lips firmed, and she spat on the gory corpse. 'This is one of the animals that took our two novices. They probably came back for more. Well, they got more than they expected.' She spat again.

'Tell me about what happened,' said Jiro. She noted that his breath was barely quickened by the violent exercise he had just undertaken.

The story was a grim one. First one novice had disappeared. That had prompted Yanagi to dispatch the letter to Goemon. The second time, masked samurai had raided the temple. The porter, an enormous woman from the isle of Shikoku, where they trained female sumo wrestlers, had died defending her post. The prioress of the temple, trying to shield her charges, had died too. The other nuns had fled. The raiders had apparently known what they had been looking for. They had seized twin novices who had been the personal acolytes of the prioress for some years now. Some had wanted to molest the rest of the nuns but had been called off by their leader. Until now, their second raid, they had had no clue as to whom the raiders represented.

'I suggest,' said Jiro, 'that you leave this place as soon as possible. In the morning I will attend to Lord Matsudaira's mansion. Is there a safe place you could all retire to?'

'There is the headquarter temple of our sect near the foot of Mount Mitake. We could go there.'

'I suggest you do. I will send word if successful. If no word comes . . .' He let his words trail off.

She bowed low to the rush mats of the room. 'We will be beholden. Please rest yourself. Food will be

119

available soon. And your bath. We will also prepare a place for you to sleep.'

'Thank you, but I had best stay awake tonight. I will need to keep watch.'

She straightened and hurried out to arrange for his food. Noting her erect carriage and smooth skin, Jiro thought that there was still much to be said for older women. This one certainly would have been worth much effort, had she not been a nun.

Trying to get the aches of the journey out of his bones, Jiro opened the paper-glazed shoji doors and stepped out onto the verandah that ran the length of the nunnery building. The grounds were immaculate but for the bodies that lay grotesquely, covered and uncovered by moonlight as clouds swept across the crescent moon. Jiro removed the sheathed long sword out of his sash and sat down on the porch. He heard the sound of footsteps in the room he had just left. Yanagi and her helpers had returned. She stepped out onto the porch, followed by another nun, who bore a tray.

'Won't you sleep?' asked Yanagi. The nun behind her handed her a pot of tea and a bowl of rice and pickled plums.

'No. There may be more of them. In any case, I will leave here in the morning, very early, to trace your novices.'

'We could stand guard for you,' she offered.

He shook his head. 'No. Though I trust you, I would rather guard myself.'

She handed him the rice bowl and a pair of chopsticks. He poured the green tea over the rice and pickles and wolfed them down. He handed the bowl back and had it refilled.

'You may go now,' said Yanagi to the other nun. 'I will keep the samurai company.' The elderly nun nodded and scurried off.

'Please do not disturb yourself. You may go to bed. I will be perfectly content to keep watch without you.'

'Would you not care for a bath?'

He grinned, and his white teeth flashed in the dark. 'I would very much like to have a bath, but it will have to wait.'

She nodded. 'Forgive me, then, for leaving you for a while. There are things I must attend to. Since the prioress was murdered, I must deal with all matters here, and we must make ready to leave as you advised. Please rest comfortably.' She bowed to the floor and left, her bare feet silent on the wooden boards.

Jiro relaxed against a pillar. It was a peculiar nunnery, he decided. The number of nuns was small, but from what he had seen of the inside, the nunnery was very rich. He heard sounds of movement inside the building, and these gradually died down as the inmates settled in for the night. The night was a balmy one. The courtyard, where the bodies of the intruders had lain, glowed with the white glimmering of the gravel that faced it. The gravel would make an effective alarm if someone tried to sneak up on him. He wondered how Okiku had arrived at this place. She had mentioned casually that she had stayed here a while looking for him, when they had been on their way to Miyako.

Thinking of her, he felt a stirring in his loins. He settled back against the pillar more comfortably. It would be as good a way as any to pass the time, he decided. He rubbed the bulge in his trousers meditatively, thinking of Okiku, and of Rosamund, and somewhat of the Chinese girl.

The sound of a sliding door broke into his reverie. He turned his head. Yanagi and three other nuns were approaching on bare feet. Their shaved heads seemed to glimmer in the dark, a complement to the courtyard. They knelt in a row before him.

'We feel that we should assist you to stay awake, since such is your wish,' Yanagi told him.

He bowed, expecting some more tea. The quartet bowed back in unison. Yanagi edged forward, still on her knees. She bowed once again and murmured, 'Excuse my clumsiness.'

He wore loose trousers over a long, by now rather stained robe. The trousers were held by long tapes that wound around his middle and helped support his swords. Long slits on the sides of the trousers allowed for easy access when a man needed to piss. Her hand worked into his trousers, loosening the tapes slightly and gently extricating his man-pole, now in full glory. It burst from its confines, pointing defiantly at the audience. One of the nuns seemed to let out a sigh.

Yanagi leaned forward, and Jiro stirred uneasily, unsure of what was expected of him.

'Please do not disturb yourself from your watch,' she said. Her companions waited silently. She lowered her head, and her breath wafted, warm and moist, over the quivering tip. Her tongue eased out from between her lips and flicked lightly at the plum-shaped head.

She nibbled lightly with her lips, then engulfed the head fully in her mouth. She sucked in the warm, fleshy shaft until he felt the tip touch the back of her throat. Well-trained muscles massaged the length, while her agile tongue pressed the shaft against her palate. She slowly withdrew her head, then sucked the length in again, bowing her body as she did so.

She kept up the exercise for a long while. Her tongue varied her movements, sipping delicately at the tip of laving the length of the shaft, while her lips held him firmly. Jiro's hips started jerking uncontrollably. Feeling his approaching climax, she withdrew her mouth. Skilful fingers pressed at the base of his balls, and the urge to spurt his seed into her waiting mouth passed with uncontrollable shivers.

She bowed to him again and withdrew, only to be replaced by another nun. She, too, used her mouth. Her plump cheeks bulged with the effort of containing his massive prick, but she persisted until she felt the squirming of his hips that proclaimed his approaching climax. Then she, too, stopped the natural process with firm fingers.

While she worked at him, Jiro tried to reciprocate, slipping a hand into her robes and squeezing a pendant breast. He tried to slide to the floor to reach the juncture of her legs with his mouth, but Yanagi stopped him.

'No, samurai-san. Please, it is not necessary. Please resume your watch. We will merely supervise your alertness.'

'But I would like to reciprocate your kindness in some fashion,' Jiro protested.

'There is no need,' she answered firmly. 'We are rewarded, and gain merit, merely through attention to duty, yours and ours.'

'However,' she continued, 'if you feel the need to employ your hands, feel free to do so, provided, of course, it does not distract you from your watch.'

123

He grunted doubtfully, but his hands resumed their exploration of the nun's upper torso. The night wore on, and the five people on the Dosojin-ji's verandah kept to their duties.

It was a sober and rather sleepy group that left the nunnery the following morning. The nuns, Yanagi had decided, would need to seek some sanctuary away from the Yoshida domain. They would travel towards Sumpu, where a major temple and nunnery of their school lay. Before leaving on his own way west, Jiro promised to send them word when they would be able to return. Behind them, the Dosojin-ji stood in the dark, empty of life and sound. He strode off, his balls hanging painfully between his thighs.

The mansion of the Matsudaira clan of Yoshida was surrounded by a grey plastered wall topped by a tiled roof-like frieze. Two footmen armed with staves and swords and wearing surcoats with the clan's crest on their backs stood before the entrance. The gates were closed, and the lack of flags and bustle seemed to indicate that the intendant was absent from his fief.

Jiro wandered past, not expecting to be challenged. He looked carefully at the wall from under the rim of his sedge hat. The mansion looked impenetrable. There was a small teahouse at the corner. Jiro sat down on one of the red-felt-covered benches and ordered a cup of tea and some of the local cakes.

He listened to the conversations around him. Most of the people were locals. The mansion was away from the great Tokaido highway. He sipped his tea and munched the cakes while listening to the conversations around him. Lord Matsudaira, it appeared, had left with his train early in the morning. He was not due for his yearly visit to the capital for some time, and since the death of the old shogun, Ieyasu, had not visited the pleasure retreat at Sampu. The townspeople were not, however, over-curious as to the whereabouts of their lord. His mere absence was cause for comment. Jiro hesitated to raise the question himself. Spying was endemic, and he wished neither to be taken for a spy nor to be exposed by one.

Slowly but methodically he made his way around the mansion, which was roughly square, though the walls had many twists and turns. They enclosed not only the lord's private apartments, but also offices and storerooms for running the fief and several gardens. Finally he spied what he had been looking for. A venerable tree bent its head over the wall, affording him the possibility of entry. From there, he was sure, he would be able to make his way into the mansion. He hoped he would be able to persuade someone to talk; beyond that, he could not think of a plan. He composed himself to wait patiently for nightfall.

The dark afforded him some protection when he returned that night. Country towns go to bed early, as Jiro knew well. He scaled the wall without difficulty, his height and youth enabling him to seize a trailing branch and haul himself up.

He leaped lightly into a tiny garden carpeted by moss. He would leave tracks, but he hoped he would not be traced beyond the wall. Okiku had told him some of the tricks of her trade, but he was too large, and in her eyes too clumsy, to be a good spy. There was only one thing for it. He bound his clothes tightly around him and slipped his long sword out of his sash. Cautiously, fearing snakes, he slipped under the floor of the mansion. As with all villas he knew, there was a distance of about a foot between the beams of the floor and the ground.

Slowly, and as silently as he could, he eased his way towards the inner house. Occasionally he would come close to an inner garden, or a passage would be blocked, and he would check his bearings or be forced to retreat. Quick peeks and cautious testing of the air for sounds and smells led him to what he thought was the right place. He would have to emerge to test his assumption. Cautiously, he tested the bottom of the mats above him until he found one that could be raised easily. The chosen mat was in a corner, an unlikely place for someone to be sleeping.

He raised the mat carefully from its rest. A faint glow from behind the paper-glazed sliding doors gave little illumination. He could sense a figure asleep in the room, near its centre. Moving very slowly, he managed to move the mat enough to make an opening. Like an enormous snake he slid out onto the floor. The mats squeaked a bit as they took his weight. He crawled across the floor on his belly until his hands encountered the silk of a quilt. He could hear the breathing now, and it was definitely that of a woman. He hesitated for a moment, but it seemed he was in the right place.

He withdrew his short sword silently. Feeling along the sleeping figure, he quickly found her neck. Her head rested on a raised wooden pillow that protected her hairdo. She slept on her back, hands and legs straight, as befits a samurai woman. Quickly he threw himself on her. His knees pinned her legs, and his weight and one arm pinned her arms to her sides. The blade of his sword rested on the smooth expanse of her throat.

She came awake with a start and tried to raise her head, but the cold tickle of steel at her throat stopped the movement. Her response startled Jiro, who had been prepared for anything from desperate resistance to a surprised scream.

In a breathy voice she whispered, 'Yes, my lord – anything you want, my lord. Thank you, oh, thank you.'

Seeing she was not about to resist, he slid off her. Keeping his blade on her throat, Jiro whispered, 'I will ask questions, and you will answer!'

This time her response was more to be expected. She stiffened in the bedclothes and made abortive movements to cover herself up with her loose robe. 'Who are you?' she whispered.

'It does not matter. I will not harm you. I only want some information.'

'I am a concubine of Lord Matsudaira of Yoshida. You and I will be killed if they find you here! Go! Go now!'

'You will definitely be killed if you do not answer my questions.'

She made an abortive move to rise, and his thick forearm prevented her. She slid her hands up and met the oak-hard muscles of his chest as he leaned over her. Her breathing quickened, and she seemed to come to a decision.

'Are you a samurai? Or a robber come to steal?'

'I am a samurai. I need to know about two women brought here secretly two days ago. Where are they? I have been sent to get them.'

'I will tell you nothing . . . ,' his arm tensed, and she felt the movement, ' . . . unless you do something for me first.'

127

Furiously he asked, 'What?' in a harsh whisper.

'This!' she said, and threw off the rest of the thin quilt that had covered her. Her light sleeping robe was open, he saw in the dim light, and her legs were spread. A darker shadow marked the juncture.

'I need you badly,' she continued. 'He leaves us alone so much. When he does come, it is rarely enough for a healthy woman like me. Come on, do it quickly. I'll not tell. My life is as forfeit as yours if they catch you here, but I'll tell you nothing unless you mount me – to my satisfaction.'

Jiro realised he was in a bind. He rapidly undid the ties of his hakama trousers and opened the robe and loincloth underneath. His massive body covered hers, and she slipped a hand down his body to the length of his magnificent prick.

He could see by the quick smile that flashed in the dark that she was pleased at his equipment. Without preliminary, he mounted her. His own juices were boiling in his balls, and he did not know how long he would be able to hold out. The nuns' treatment made him almost lose his charge then and there, as he slipped into a slick, moist channel that parted before his onslaught.

Out of politeness, he came to rest, but for a mere second, when their hairs merged.

'No – don't wait!' she urged him, slapping his muscular buttocks. He withdrew and pushed forward again, then started riding her hard in earnest. Their breathing grew harsh as his prick was enveloped with her marvellous cunt. Her legs rose and clutched him to her. His lips sought hers, partly for the pleasure it gave him, partly out of fear that she might cry out and give them away. He insinuated a hand between their bodies and squeezed a broad, flat breast. The erect nipple pressed against his palm. She stuck a hand through his trousers and gently fingered his hairy ball bag and asshole.

The last move proved too much for Jiro. His movements became frenzied, almost panicked, as a gush of sperm shot out from the depths of his balls and flooded her interior. She moaned in distress as she tried to match his climax. Her pubes jerked stickily against him, as she ground her clit between their pelvises in a mute search for satisfaction.

To her surprise, the giant lying on her did not stop his movements. He rested for a few seconds, then commenced his movements again, as if struck by a demon. She clutched him again in delight as he reamed her flooded channel. She felt beneath her. The cheeks of her ass and the bedding beneath were soaked with his copious spending. His massive cock began to jerk inside her, and this time his pumping was met by pumping of her own as her delayed climax merged with his.

Again, he did not stop moving. After a short rest he started pumping at her in earnest again. She was in a delirium of pleasure. His cock scored the length of her channel, plunging into her deepest recesses. She gasped into his mouth and would have called out her pleasure for all to hear but for his lips on her own. Instead she bit at his plunging tongue and was bitten in return.

Much later he finally let her go. She lay supine in the dark, her legs spread in exhaustion, while he lay beside her. She idly fingered the pool of juices between her legs and mopped her sopping curls with a careless finger. Her other hand gently milked his now softened prick, smearing his muscular belly with their mingled juices.

'I'll tell you what you want to know now. We must hurry, I do not want you to be caught. I did not care before, but now . . .'

'Where is Lord Matsudaira?'

She stiffened. Her loyalty to her lord still motivated her. 'Why?' she demanded, afraid of assassination.

'He has kidnapped several novices from a nunnery. They are the disciples of a friend of mine, and I am going to steal them back.'

She relaxed. Her lord's predilections were well known. Though she was far from being his favourite and was rarely called into his presence, his peculiar tastes were difficult to hide, particularly in the House of Women. A knight about to rescue some maidens, like a character from a Chinese story, appealed to her emotions.

'I'm sorry,' she said simply. 'He has left, taking the two new ones with him.'

For a moment, Jiro was angry at having been tricked; then the delight of the situation occurred to him. He laughed quietly. 'Where has the Lord Matsudaira gone?'

'To Miyako, I believe.'

'Do you know where he is to stay?'

'I think he stays at a place called the Sanjo, in the city. I have never been there, of course. Do you know Miyako? How I wish you could tell me about it . . .' She sounded wistful, a country wren in a gilded cage. He kissed her sorrowfully.

'Is there a room where he works, stores documents?'

'He has a study where he sometimes works at administrative matters.' She described the location, which was not far – not surprising, since the House of Women was traditionally the most secure area of a mansion.

As he dressed, his mind whirled with speculations. The matter would have to end in Miyako. He would find the girls there and fulfil his promise to Yanagi. Then he would be free to deal with the shogun's problems. But first he would have to search the office for any clues.

She bowed low at his departure, sudden as his arrival through the tatami mat. She was never to know his name.

He left the mansion much later that night. The study did not seem to have yielded any clues. There were no incriminating documents. The only suspicious items that caught his attention were several lengths of peculiar black cord, each knotted into the same intricate shape. The cords were impregnated with a black grainy substance he could not identify in the pale glimmer of moonlight in which he searched. He took one, hoping it would mean something to someone. Not until he was well on his way, riding a hired horse furiously toward Miyako and home, did the significance of the cord occur to him.

Chapter 8

The palanquin bearers put down their burden and knelt. Together they opened the mat that screened the rider from the gaze of passing crowds. Goemon uncurled himself and stepped out. He was facing a blank door of heavy planks overshadowed by the eaves of an imposing house. He approached, and the door opened a crack.

'Goemon, of the house of Saizo,' he said quietly.

The door swung open, and he was ushered in by a heavyset porter, who bowed and said, 'Welcome, welcome.'

Goemon proceeded through a short passageway that debouched onto a fairy scene. A small garden was lit by a multitude of lanterns. They illuminated bushes and small trees rising in well-designed steps to create the illusion of a rocky valley through which meandered a small stream. The pathway before his feet was paved with gravel, which crunched as he walked. The path curved around a pile of rocks after several paces, and Goemon found himself facing a well-lit entryway.

A maid dressed in a white robe ornamented with azaleas bowed and called out, 'Welcome!' in a high-pitched voice. He entered and dropped his straw sandals while stepping up onto the wooden floor of the house itself. Above him he could hear the sound of laughter and the strings of a samisen as a clear woman's voice sang a ballad.

He climbed the stairs and faced a closed sliding door. Another maid knelt at the entrance. She bowed to him and waited while he checked his costume. Satisfied that all was right, she slid open the door. He entered and knelt on the mats at the entrance. A heavyset man, who was sitting near the entrance, rose and approached, and then bowed on his knees to Goemon in return.

'Goemon, of the house of Saizo. My master bade me come before his departure.' Goemon extracted a folded sheet of paper from the breast of his robe. It bore one line and the red stamp of Saizo's seal. 'In my stead, with my regrets,' it said.

The heavyset man bowed. 'I am Rokuro. I am very pleased to have you. Did your master convey anything...?'

'I am afraid not,' said Goemon in a low voice. 'He merely informed me before... that you would be meeting here, asked me to replace him. He said that he had regretfully given you an evasive answer because of his health but that he wished to indicate support for your venture by asking me to attend instead. I was his clerk for many years, and I established a branch office in Kanazawa.' The little bit of embroidery would be safe enough, Goemon thought. Saizo being Saizo would never have

133

mentioned anything more to his clerk.

'Do you know what we are engaged in?' asked Rokuro.

'Of course. I understand you are a combine that supplies goods for the Honourable Hall in Miyako. Since other arrangements could not be made in so short a time, I have undertaken to represent my master.'

Rokuro gazed for a time at the young, honest-seeming face before him, then moved aside, still on his knees, with a smile. 'Please join us,' he said. 'There will still be another to come. You might find him disturbing, though interesting. He is a southern barbarian merchant. Have you ever met such?'

'I have had the honour,' responded Goemon, thinking wistfully of Rosamund's curves. He sat down before one of the tables. The room was elaborately, even garishly decorated. A Chinese scroll depicting Li Po admiring the moon hung in an alcove, a lush flower arrangement before it. A gilt doll from a temple in the Kanto looked down. Other objects could be seen around. The tables, set for about sixteen, were arranged as an open square facing the entrance. Twelve men sat around the outer rim of the square. Opposite them were several entertainers. One of the entertainers was playing the samisen. Another, dressed more elaborately than the others, with multiple pins in her elaborate hairdo, was sitting opposite the head of the table, where two empty seats were kept.

A pretty-eyed girl in a robe of iris design poured sake from a blue-ware bottle into a tiny cup. These cups were only lately becoming popular. Goemon drank the warm sake, flipped the dregs out of the cup, and offered it gallantly to the entertainer. She giggled coyly behind her hand, tried to refuse, but eventually acquiesced. He poured her a drink, which she sipped. A loud burst of laughter attracted his attention. When he turned back, the cup was empty.

The door slid open. A massive frame stood at the entrance. Goemon recognised him as the giant, dark-skinned captain he had seen with Jiro. The man bowed, still standing, and Goemon thought him a trifle shorter than Jiro. Then he straightened and Goemon changed his mind. Kneeling on the floor, with no trace of reaction at the foreigner's rudeness in not kneeling, Rokuro greeted his guest, then rose to show him his seat.

They sat at the head of the table, and Rokuro clapped his hands for silence.

'I am Rokuro. We meet here as a consortium to convey our goods to Mikayo. I present the Captain DaSilva. He has received a licence from the governor at Osaka and from the military government to visit Miyako and enjoy the sights and shrines. He will be joining us and also possibly offering some of his goods for the Hall's inspection and appreciation. Unfortunately, the honourable captain does not speak Japanese, and so I will be forced to interpret for him.'

Goemon was not sure of the truth of the latter statement. The southern barbarian's eyes seemed to follow the talk too closely.

'We will be leaving in a few days' time, as soon as all the goods are ready. We will be travelling together, so I beg of you to be in time. We of Osaka must make a good showing.

'I propose a toast: to our success in a pleasant and profitable journey. Bottoms up.'

'Bottoms up,' the rest of the company echoed.

Goemon purposely caught the entertainer's eye and winked. She giggled and hid her mouth.

The next two hours were a tiring blur to Goemon. They ate and drank incessantly. The entertainers played endless drinking and word games. They laughingly evaded the clutching hands of the drinking men, while contriving to drink as little themselves as they could. Several times groups of entertainers rose to dance or act skits and playlets, both the stately court ones and the more bumptious and raunchy country dances.

At one point during the evening Goemon rose and did the obligatory round, introducing himself and drinking with all his future companions. The foreigner, he saw, had had much to drink. He was attempting to fondle the chief entertainer, and she suffered, not without embarrassment, having his hand in her robe. Goemon's arrival with a cup and a bottle was an excuse for her to escape, and she was replaced by a less experienced apprentice.

Goemon bowed and introduced himself. DaSilva nodded and grunted. His full attention was on the young entertainer. She was giggling artificially while trying to avoid his hands. Goemon poured some sake and offered the cup. The giant gulped it down and blinked owlishly at Goemon.

'Tiny cups and tiny women. I love it. Love it, you hear? Both have fire. Why, this little wine is stronger than the wines of Jerez, and this little thing will please me more than...' He stopped and looked at the entertainer at his side. 'This isn't the one!' he roared. 'Where is she?'

The strange words were incomprehensible to both the entertainer and Goemon, but Rokuro bent over quickly from his seat.

'Is there anything the matter DaSilva Captain?' he asked in his halting Portuguese.

'Yes,' muttered the dark man. 'There was another one of these ... one with gold hairpins. Ah! There she is!' He spotted the chief entertainer on the other side of the room talking to another of the merchants. 'No matter,' he slurred. 'I'll flutter both of 'em.'

Rokuro's Portuguese was too slow for him to sort out whether DaSilva meant the merchant as well. The giant staggered to his feet, sending the table rolling. The chief entertainer hurried towards them. Her mouth was still smiling, but there was a crease to her brow that her heavy white makeup could not conceal.

'C'mere, you little wench. Let's find another room and I'll flutter you right now.'

For a moment the geisha looked at him quietly, her eyes glowing. Then, for apparently her profession had taught her the need for foreign languages as well, she managed to make out the meaning of his words.

'Sit down, you ugly barbarian,' she said vehemently. 'I am not a whore for you to take and ... take!' In her fury, her Portuguese failed her.

She continued in a mixture of Portuguese and Japanese while the guests made a poor attempt at appearing to ignore the whole scene while listening avidly to the exchange. 'I ... will ... not ... have ... anything ... to ... do ... with ... you!' She accompanied each word with a jab of her finger at the region of his chest, which was also the height of her eyes.

The captain, surprised, stumbled back while simultaneously reaching for her. He tripped and fell

137

with a crash, his head landing next to Goemon's surprised face.

'I'll kill the bitch!' he muttered. His face turned darker with blood and he made to rise. Goemon lent a helping hand at the captain's shoulder, and the man collapsed in a heap. The geisha, her breast still heaving rapidly, looked closely at Goemon for a moment, then spun rapidly on her heels and glided out of the dining room.

Servants came in and made the captain comfortable in another room. The party wore on. The next time Goemon saw the chief entertainer she had changed her dress and came in to dance a stately court dance, accompanied by three of her apprentices, girls in their early teens, too young to be trusted with appearing on their own as entertainers.

The party was winding down when Goemon made to leave. He thanked Rokuro and made arrangements to have Saizo's shipment of tea arrive at the common meeting point. Rokuro was responsible for arranging porters and would enjoy the profits of the middle man from managing the affair.

Goemon stepped out into the cool night air. He leisurely put on his sandals, which had been placed conveniently, toes out, by the maid, and stepped out into the garden. The figure of a young girl was waiting there. She bowed wordlessly and handed him a folded note tied to a wisteria branch. In the light of the lantern he could make out a stamp in purplish ink that read, 'Ohei.'

The girl waited until he indicated he would follow. She led him through the garden and several staircases and corridors to a small room. In the distance he could hear the sounds of the party. He entered and knelt, bowing as he did.

'I wanted to thank you for helping me earlier,' said a voice from his side.

He turned and repeated the bow. The geisha was sitting there. Her makeup was simpler now, and she wore a simpler robe, tied with a plain rose-coloured sash.

'It was nothing,' he said politely.

'No, please. The pressure grip you used paralysed him. Otherwise, I'm afraid my reputation would have suffered. Such an animal, not knowing how to behave . . .' For a moment anger showed in her voice.

'If you have the time,' she continued in a calmer voice, 'I would be happy to show my gratitude.'

Intrigued, Goemon bowed and said, 'Really, there is no need – but of course, my time is yours.'

She smiled and bowed gracefully, then clapped her hands. The sliding doors at the farther side of the room slid open as two of the geisha's apprentices, hidden till then by the doors, bowed at the entrance. The room beyond was lit by several lamps. In its middle was a large mosquito net suspended from the corners of the room. It made a large gauze box, in which lay a wide, fluffy pallet. The geisha rose, and her sash, which had not been tied behind, slipped off. Her pale robe was now held simply by a scarf tied on her middle by a granny knot. He rose and walked after her swaying form. As she ducked under the net, one of the apprentices began to play a samisen softly.

She bade Goemon sit on the pallet, and rapidly loosened his sash and opened his robes. She stroked the bulge in his loincloth for a moment, then undid and removed the garment. His cock rose in proud erection. She smiled at Goemon momentarily, then bent and fondled the silky-feeling member. She

139

played with it for a while, banging the head against his belly, caressing it with her cheek, sniffing delicately at its masculine smell. Her tongue licked out once or twice, to taste the salty extrusion that appeared at the tip.

Goemon sat perfectly still, letting her practise her art. She moved forward, and her knees rose under his armpits, while she squatted over the erect staff. She twined her arms about his neck, softly biting the skin, while her hairy cunt hovered just above his prick head with perfect control.

Undulating slowly, she rubbed the barest tip of his member against the length of her slit. The going was rough at first. Her hairs scratched against the sensitive tip. Gradually the going got easier as her lubricating fluids smoothed the path through the forest.

She joined her mouth to his and slowly let her rump down the length of his shaft. He could clearly feel the progress as her juicy nether lips greedily swallowed his shaft, inch by slow inch. At the same time she applied hungry lips to his own. Her mouth had been freshened by an infusion, and he tasted the merest essence of flowers as her tongue probed his mouth, then retreated before his own lingual onslaught.

Her ass reached bottom, and she rested there for a second, careful not to place her weight on his thighs. She seemed boneless down below, her pelvic bones insulated above his by the warm softness of her ass.

She rose again, more slowly than she had descended. Goemon restrained an urge to force her down on his demanding prick. Without releasing the head of his cock from her confining cunt, she swayed several times from side to side, then let herself down again.

This time when she rose, she left more of the shaft within her as she swayed again. She repeated the motion until her swaying dance on his cock was performed with their sopping hairs entwined. He marvelled at her muscular control. Even when she rocked tightly in his lap, he could not feel the hard pressure of her bones. Her dance slowed, and her rocking pelvis came to a stop, while her tongue still wrestled his in the joined caverns of their mouths.

Now she started constricting the muscles of her inner channel rhythmically, her hips almost stationary. Her powerful internal muscles milked the length of his fleshy pole, the muscular spasm travelling the length of the imprisoned shaft.

The squeezing sensation was more than Goemon could bear. His balls contracted once in warning; then he flooded her insides with jets of warm sperm that watered her feverish insides and ran out onto his lap.

He looked at her in apology for his haste. She merely smiled, and her inner muscles increased their milking tempo. Rather than shrinking inside her, his inflamed member held its stiffness. Her eyes closed to mere slits, and her mouth opened languidly while she rode. Her hands clutched his back, probing into and easing his muscles. He longed to squeeze her breasts, but in their position could do little but slide his hands down and finger her buttocks and the little button of her anus. She sighed gratefully.

When he was perfectly stiff, she swayed up once more. This time she stood erect and changed position. Raising the skirts of her robe to expose her perfect backside, she stood before him for a moment. He admired the pale gold of her buttocks, split by a perfect line. She bent forward from the waist, and her cunt was exposed in its entire length. The lips were tiny and well formed, framed by a fringe of black straight hair, now dripping with his moisture. The slit was tiny and showed as a mere darker line between the lips. She dropped the skirts of her robe for a moment and modestly wiped herself with a sheet of soft paper handed her by a novice. Raising her robe one more time, she allowed him another glance at her perfect rear before squatting and impaling herself once more.

This time she slid forward and down onto his shaft without a pause. Reaching behind her, she sought his hands. She slid his palms sensuously over the smoothness of her ass, not forgetting to direct his digital attention to the portal of her rear opening and the juncture of their flesh at her lower mouth. Then she brought his hands forward, first to titillate her cunt, lingering long over the tiny clitoris, then touching and fondling his balls gently.

Goemon found this guided tour of them both tremendously exciting. He had to restrain himself forcefully from plunging ahead into this delightful and insightful creature. Instead he fell delightedly into her mood, following each of her moves to perfection. Now she slid his palms up the length of her smooth belly. The muscles quivered slightly as he passed. She started rocking forward and back, exciting his prick as it dug deeper into her, then retreated. She came to rest on her breasts. They hung smoothly beneath her ribcage, not too large, but soft and full. She squeezed his palms on her erect nipples, circled the areolas with their fingers. For a moment she crushed his fingers into the twin mounds of flesh; then she smoothed the damage away with broad sweeps of her palms. Finally she just left his hands on her breasts. Her hands descended to support her on the floor, and she leaned forward, face to the pallet, passively awaiting his pleasure.

Goemon did not need any more encouragement. His juice was boiling in his balls, and the prolonged kneeling was becoming uncomfortable. He rose to his knees, his cock into her to its full length, and launched himself forward. Her body shook as it absorbed the blow, and she moaned low in her throat.

Grasping her tits firmly, Goemon set to work. His hips shuttled back and forth as he crushed her beneath his weight. His cock frothed as it churned her passive insides. He licked and nibbled at the smooth skin of her back, tasting the powder with which she had whitened her shoulders. He was gasping audibly now, his eyes practically starting out of his head.

Now she added a new element. As he drove forward, she constricted her cunt walls. Though her muscles were not as powerful as Rosamund's, they were well trained and provided an additional friction to his engorged member.

Wordless sounds emerged from his mouth as he threaded her opening in a frenzy. She lay passively beneath him as his sperm rose in his balls and splashed out into her interior. Only the muscles of her cunt told of the reaction to the inundation. He clasped her to him forcefully, melting into her soft ass, as his frenzied charge became a spasmodic jerking, and her twitching inner muscles milked him dry.

*

'You are tired,' said Ohei with consideration when he had recovered and they had drunk some tea. 'Would you like some entertainment? It is very funny.'

Amazed at himself, Goemon agreed. They tied each other's robes carelessly, and she led him through several rooms. Light spilled through the crack of one of the doors. Grunting sounds came from within. She motioned him to silence, mischief glinting in her eyes. They knelt together near the fusuma door, and she gently eased it open a crack.

DaSilva was lying flat on his back. Crouched over him was a female figure. It was a young, plump girl Goemon did not recognise. She was raising and lowering her rump. Her ass was caught in DaSilva's big hands, and Goemon could see the length of the crack, the tiny bud of her asshole, the gooey crack of her cunt, distended now by the thickness of the captain's cock. That instrument, darker than the rest of him, almost black, was glistening with the twosome's juices. The captain was grunting and snorting while the girl worked away at him.

Suddenly he picked her up entirely from him, the long prick flopping down on his muscular belly, and reversed the girl. He laid her on his chest, and his hand forced her head onto the stiff member. Her rosebud mouth opened, and she engulfed the cock with an effort. The captain pumped for a while at her distended face. He stiffened, and a ripple ran the length of the black staff. The girl's cheeks bulged, and Goemon thought he could see tears in her eyes. She swallowed several times, but not fast enough. Driblets of white juice spilled out of the corner of her mouth and ran down her chin.

At last the pumping stopped. DaSilva raised her in

the air again. Amazingly, his stiff rammer was still at attention. He positioned the girl on it once again, and she wearily began her up-and-down motion once more.

Ohei drew Goemon off, a sleeve muffling her mouth. When they were several rooms away she allowed her giggling to escape.

'Such a boor,' she said contemptuously. 'I had heard he knew nothing of sex. Did you see how he went at that poor girl? It might be fun for a while, but with no variation...! That is why they get him the cheapest whores from the licensed quarter. He doesn't know the difference anyway!'

They crept back to her room. Goemon noticed he had been affected pleasantly by the sight they had seen. Indeed, he had thought to throw Ohei on the mat floor and have her right next to the captain. Good manners and a certain caution had prevailed. But now... She looked on approvingly as he parted his robe.

'Goemon, may I ask a favour?'

'Of course.' A short nap had refreshed him considerably, and he was idly considering her pale face.

'You are of course my guest, and it is unmannerly to impose...' Her voice trailed off.

'No, not at all. You have been extremely kind.'

She drew a breath. 'I have four apprentices. They are really good for little but some music, and helping me prepare myself, fetch things, and so on. Soon, however, there will be customers asking after them. Now, besides the need to recover some of my investment in them – you have no idea how much it costs to get a good girl these days – I must ensure

145

they do not affect my reputation adversely.'

'And?' prompted Goemon, not comprehending.

'Well, some men pay well for virgins, so on the one hand that is worth thinking of. On the other hand, I do not purvey women for sleeping with. There are houses for that. So if men are going to sleep with them after a party, they must be accomplished in what they do. To preserve *my* reputation, you understand.' She bowed slightly to him. 'Could you perhaps take their virginities for me? I realise it is a bother, but it's so much better than doing it mechanically.'

Goemon nodded, speechless. 'How many did you say there were?' he finally managed to ask.

'Only four. I'm afraid I have to admit I cannot afford more yet.'

'Bring them on,' he said weakly. But his confidence rose as the first apprentice knelt before him. She was a tiny thing, dressed in a pale pink underrobe. The translucent fabric shadowed the lines of her body. Without rising from the cushion he untied the knot on her sash and opened her robe. Her breasts were relatively flat, with large areolas and flat, wide nipples. He teased each nipple with thumb and forefinger while the young maiko looked down shyly. He slid his hands down her smooth, slightly plump torso to the narrow part of her hips, then past them to the swell of her thighs. When both hands were on her knees, he parted them gently.

Now his hands travelled up the slim white flesh of her inner thighs. He parted her legs further until his thumbs could reach the lips of cunt. They were lightly framed by a downy fringe of hair. He ran his thumb up and down the length of the external lips. This time she parted her thighs of her own volition.

146

Though her eyes were still looking down shyly, he could feel the tension gather in her. The inner lips of her cunt were longer than the outer ones, and he teased them open, to be rewarded with the soft, sweet, juicy petals of her inside flower. He teased the entrance to the enchanting channel for a while, watching the effect of his motions on the girl's face. Her eyes seemed glazed, and she moistened her lips repeatedly.

Distracted by a motion, Goemon raised his head. He now had an audience. Three other young girls looked on with interest as his fingers teased at their co-worker. He parted the lips gently and sought the entrance. It was blocked by a taut hymen, and the girl stirred uneasily at the unfamiliar sensation. He eased his hands away from her cunt, and the girl looked up for the first time. It seemed from her look that she was disappointed.

Goemon laid a hand on either side of her body. He bent his trunk backward until he lay flat on his back.

'Open it!' he said to the girl. She reached with two hands and flipped back his robe. His lightly confined prick, which had made a distinct lump in the cloth, sprung erect. The girl took in a quick breath. The other three giggled in embarrassment – or perhaps it was fear – and covered their mouths. Ohei hissed them to quiet.

Goemon lifted the girl into the air while unfolding his legs and dragged her body along his. The smooth slide of her breasts, belly, and thighs along the length of his prick raised an ooze of juice that tickled her skin. Her legs were splayed on either side of his hips. He paused there for a moment while she looked deep into his eyes. Her own had very thick epicanthic folds, which made them look like slits in a

147

doll's face.

He raised her higher until she was poised vertically over his supine body. Manipulating her in the air, he searched with the head of his cock for her virgin opening. There was a whisper of command from Ohei. A slim, soft hand took hold of his prick as one of the other maiko peered closely for her friend's opening and guided Goemon's cock into it. He jigged his hips up experimentally a couple of times. Sure now that he was well seated, he pulled her suddenly to him. She let out a sound, part cry, part moan, part delighted sigh. His flesh sword struck up into her channel, tearing and rupturing at the first, then expanding an unused but well-designed channel. Her insides responded quickly. The head of his prick pushed waves of sensation into her. She collapsed, a limp doll, onto the hardness of his chest.

She was light enough for him to move her back and forth while she recovered. The going was hard at first, but the droplets of blood lubricated her somewhat, and then her natural reaction to the pleasant pressence of an intruder in her midst brought about a shower of juices. Gradually she started moving with him. She pushed her palms against his chest, and the delicate feel of her hands stimulated his movements. Her eyes seemed to glaze, the lids drooped, and she gave several sighs as she was overcome by her first orgasm. Her thighs clenched over his hips, and she shuddered to a climax over him.

He looked at the second one. She was slimmer than the first maiko. She had larger, fuller breasts and a thicker bush between her legs. He led her to her friend, the deflowered one, while caressing her shoulders and neck.

'Would you like that?' he whispered, just for her ears.

Shyly she nodded.

'Kneel down and put your head on her belly. She will help hold you.'

The maiko did as she was told. Goemon looked with pleasure at her young buttocks. They were plump and a light golden colour. The vertical slit between her buns was tight and well shaped and, when he parted her knees, displayed an exquisite pursed asshole and tempting long, narrow pussy lips. His cock was still wet from the first girl's blood and internal fluids. He knelt behind the kneeling girl. His hands slid the length of her body, from bulging ass along her sides, to her plump hanging breasts. He squeezed them a trifle roughly, and she moaned in protest. He licked her smooth back with his tongue, which made her squirm and giggle. Again his aim was helped by a slim hand that slid past hanging balls to the shaft and aimed him true. He slid his left hand forward to grasp her shoulder at the soft joint with the neck. His right gathered both breasts in one handful, pinching the nipples together; then he lunged mercilessly forward.

The soft cushion of the supine girl supported the weight of both Goemon and the girl he was in. Her channel was smooth and wet, and soon Goemon found himself gliding up her at an increasing tempo. She writhed under him, protesting or not, he did not know nor care. Grunts came from both of them, and perhaps from the girl who served as cushion as well.

Goemon realised he would not be able to make all four. He was about to reach his climax, and there was no doubt in his mind that he would be good for little before morning. He was conscious of Ohei's face hovering over his. It was easy for her to tell that Goemon had lost his control. His teeth were clenched, and his hips moved almost automatically, pistoning in and out of the girl's bruised cunt.

Ohei's head descended. She bit viciously at his ear to bring him to his senses, while her thumb dug into the spot behind his balls. He almost shrieked with pain, but the same pain brought him to his senses, and the continuing pressure under his balls relieved him of much of the pressure in his balls. He collapsed on the two girls. Ohei and the other two maiko rolled him off. He lay there breathing heavily.

He knelt before Ohei in apology when he had recovered.

'I am not worthy –' he started, but she broke into his sentence.

'No, no, Goemon. It is my fault, making you work without enjoying the fruits of your labours. Please forgive me.'

He laughed quietly and shook his head. 'There is nothing to forgive. You were quite right. I am ready to continue. Please.'

She bowed in acquiescence and ordered the third girl forward, then whispered some words in her ear. The girl leaned over Goemon's lap and sucked in his limp, moist prick. Her tiny mouth set quickly to work, inexpertly but enthusiastically licking and sucking for all she was worth. His prick responded, swelling in her mouth to a pleasing stiffness. The girl turned to her mistress questioningly.

Ohei bent and checked on the result of the novice's work. She nodded in approval, then sucked in the rampant length several times as a finishing touch.

She placed the girl's head on her own lap, then leaned forward and grasped her ankles and pulled them to her. The girl was now folded in half. Her almost hairless purse was displayed prominently between her thighs. Below them the tiny bud of her asshole seemed to pulse in anticipation.

Ohei nodded at Goemon. 'If you please, Goemon, she is ready. Please do not try to make her dew descend. There is plenty of time for that, and I would not like you to become exhausted.'

He nodded and knelt before the girl for a moment. She peeped at him shyly over her exposed sex. The sight of her complete exposure to his pleasure brought on an added flush to his rampant lust. He bent his cock with one hand while feeling her virginal slit with the other. He adjusted his aim carefully. The tip lodged barely into the taut opening while he wet her slightly with gradual motions of his member. Her thighs were quivering with the strain of her position. He launched himself forward gently but inexorably. This time he clearly heard her cry out as her hymen tore, just as he felt the sudden giving way of the restraining membrane. He paused for a moment at the entrance to give her some time to recover, then forced his way up her virginal cavern. She restrained her cries, but her eyeballs were hidden by tightened lids. He rested again at the limits of his penetration, then withdrew slowly.

The entrance was now easier for both of them, and he set to work, pumping slowly and easily at her prominent pussy. Her breathing eased for a while; then its tempo increased as the pleasure of the sensation began reaching her. He leaned forward to look at her face, but Ohei intercepted his move and

151

presented her own lips to his. She sucked hungrily at his mouth, while his hands squeezed and pinched at her breasts and then at the smaller ones of her apprentice.

The girl beneath him twitched and gasped, and he felt sympathetic vibrations start between his own thighs. Ohei, on the lookout for these signs, released the girl's thighs, rose from the couple, and gently decoupled them. She stood for a moment with Goemon, looking at the exhausted girl as she lay on the mat. Seemingly with a will of its own, the girl's hand crept to her cunt. It dipped into the opening, as if to assess the damage, and the girl smiled at the feeling of the open passageway. Hesitantly, the hand then stroked the length of the slim, hairless cunt, coming to rest on the clitoris, where it rubbed hungrily. With an embarrassed start the girl removed her hand and opened her eyes. Goemon and Ohei smiled at her, and she smiled tentatively back, as the two turned to the last virgin.

She was lying on her back, stripped naked, anticipation gleaming in her eyes. Her hand had been dipping between her thighs, and both her pussy and her fingers glinted with moisture.

'She's a randy one,' commented Ohei. 'She'll not go far in our profession. Too involved physically. For the meantime she'll do, though I do believe you've arrived not a moment too soon for her.'

She knelt by the girl and adjusted her position, laying her on her side, the upper thigh drawn up to her full breast.

'Mount her like that,' commanded the geisha. She stripped herself and lay down facing her apprentice. It was clear that Ohei intended to be more than a spectator this time. The other three novices looked on interested.

The maiko's cunt hairs lay flat on her extended thigh, and her bent leg allowed him easy access. For a moment he fingered her soft, mossy grotto. It was slick with her juices, and the hymen was unnoticeable, perhaps because she had fingered herself so often.

Without much ado Goemon straddled her extended leg and presented his cock at her opening. Eagerly she jerked her hips back at him as he pushed forward. His lance slid into her without any hindrance. She sighed happily and pushed back as his shaft raged forward. As he moved he could feel Ohei's hand on the juncture, urging them on. She rose and reversed her position, presenting her full cunt to the novice's willing mouth. Goemon watched entranced as the woman's rich cunt was licked thoroughly by the excited girl. His own motions became frenzied. The girl uttered a muffled cry, and her body tensed and stretched out against him. Her channel flowed with moisture as she came in slight regular tremors, then recommenced its pumping motion.

Goemon set his teeth. This time, he knew, he would burst if he could not climax. His hands gripped the girl, one searching for her breast, the other gripping her upper thigh. He closed his eyes. Only the soft sensation of her liquid cunt against his rampant cock had any meaning. The surge began rising in him, when suddenly the girl was violently wrenched from his grasp. He opened his eyes in rage, ready to strike out in frustration. The three other novices were pulling the mewling body of the fourth from beneath him. He lunged forward, only to find himself on Ohei. She spread her legs and expertly fielded his ramming cock. Without breaking the rhythm of his moves she urged him on. Her own eyes closed in pleasure as he rammed home. His movements became a blur as his passion was loosened. Jet after jet of thick come splashed from his balls and flooded her thirsty cunt. He was conscious that she called out with him, just as he was conscious of the four novices in two pairs, head to tail, laving one another with their mouths, and he knew that she had climaxed with him for the first time.

In travel dress, broad sedge hat and gaiters, Goemon arrived at the meeting point, where the train of porters was gathered. After a period of confusion that seemed to last the morning, they were all loaded. The long line of porters, pack horses, and palanquins wound along the road. Goemon's sharp eyes noted that several of the porters seemed to have erect bearings that seemed to indicate that they had had other occupations in the recent past. They were all armed with short swords, rather unusual for the short trip to Miyako, even though the goods they carried – lacquerware, tea, silk, imported pottery, and other goods – were valuable. Among the packs were the possessions of the foreign merchants and the figure of Captain DaSilva, riding a horse. These two were heavily guarded.

Goemon knew he would have no chance of examining all the baggage, but being close to it was a point in his favour. At least he knew something was going on, and where. And, he smiled to himself, by the morrow he would be seeing his friends again.

Chapter 9

Okiku's movements were more cautious this time. She crept carefully under Mizuno-no-kami's mansion, noting the traps that were laid in her way. He had scattered small bamboo splinters under the floor, presumably poisoned. Other barbs stuck downward from the floor, which would have entangled her clothes as she crept about under the floorboards. Just like a real rat, she grinned to herself.

Eventually she found a loose tatami mat, which she managed to pry up delicately. Carefully she drew herself up into the villa and set to work. She prowled carefully through the vast expanse of the building. She noted traps here, too. Ankle-breaker studs stuck up out of many corridor floors. Some rooms could not be entered except by walking across nightingale boards, which squeaked musically when one passed.

Overall, however, she was struck by the musty

air of neglect, even poverty, that afflicted the mansion. Many of the fusuma doors, and even the ceiling panels of the rooms, appeared to be elaborately decorated with delicate paintings and scrollwork carvings. Light from the outside allowed her but a glimpse of their beauty as she searched for the elusive chest. She came at last to an inner room that appeared well used. There she found a large desk and several Chinese document chests, all locked. She looked around and smiled. Success at last. On the tokonoma niche rested a heavy iron-bound chest. The tatami mat before it seemed somehow uneven to Okiku.

Carefully, she extracted some tools from her sash. Bearclaw hooks went on her wrists, and she prepared several spikes. As silently as she could, she climbed up a supporting pillar, far from the tokonoma. She dug the claws into the upper side of the beam that ran the length of the wall, then hung by her hands. Working the claws successively and swinging her weight from hand to hand, she made her way along the wall, then along the perpendicular wall.

Now she was suspended by her claws directly above the tokonoma and the chest it contained. Holding on with one claw, she fumbled at her belt for the spikes. The strain of the claw on her wrist caused a rictus of pain on her face. The spike dropped from her hand and landed with a soft thud on the mat. She froze, listening intently. The villa was as quiet as before. Again she secured a spike. She drove it cautiously into the beam, again hiding the scar of entry in the upper, hidden side of the beam. Another spike was driven in, then another before she was satisfied.

A silk rope, light but strong, was hitched to the three spikes. She hoped they would hold. She made several loops with her teeth and one free hand in the cord before letting it down. Sweat poured down her face and was absorbed into her mask while she worked.

Cautiously she tested her makeshift sling before trusting her weight to it. The cord held, and she relaxed gratefully onto the support of the cord. Her left hand was completely numb, and her shoulder ached with a sharp burning pain. She rested for a while.

When she had recovered, she lowered herself until she was squatting on the cord, at the level of the chest. Opening the locks was child's play for her. They were old and cumbersome. She extracted document cases, searching for Satsuki's name. A tiny cage of fireflies, hidden in her pack for the purpose, provided her only illumination.

With a long folding bamboo probe she checked each drawer for hidden compartments. The document, when she found it, was in plain view. It rested on a pile of similar boxes, each one apparently made to order, each one apparently with papers of Mizuno's different dependants. The pink azaleas on the cover were a perfect indicator.

She opened the box and scanned its contents. Under a pile of love letters and poems and a document assigning the owner rights in several rice fields in the province of Musashi, she found the deed to 'a plot of ground and the house built thereon in the Gion ward of Miyako.' She expelled a deep breath of relief.

Under the love letters was a further document, a folded sheet of paper tied with a peculiar black cord.

The cord was tied in a tie known as a chrysanthe-mum-leaf knot. The paper bore a single, rather trite line of poetry. She puzzled over the cord for a while; then understanding dawned, and she laughed silently. She cut off a small length of the paper cord. Some of the impregnated gunpowder scattered out. Ingenious, she thought, using a slow match as a document tie. And a message.

Restoring everything to its place, she climbed back up the rope, pausing for a moment to admire the fusuma panels; then their import struck her. Azaleas, in glowing natural colours, were painted on the panels. The pinks, blues, purples, and reds, somewhat larger than life, smiled back at her. She had found the kuge at last.

Okiku leaped lightly from the roof of Gojo-no-Satsuki's dwelling. She landed silently outside the lady's habitual sleeping room. With a special tool she eased up the amado shutters and slipped inside. She froze. From behind the half-open shoji she could hear a sound she knew only too well.

Gojo-no-Satsuki was groaning ecstatically as a man grunted and panted over her. Okiku could hear the slither of the two sweating bodies on the bedding. For a moment she was furious. Her arm still ached, she had gotten away with what Gojo-no-Satsuki had requested, and here was the slut enjoying herself. At the same time she was aware that the strenuous exercise, and the sounds from the room before her, were acting on her in an entirely expected way. And she had not had a man for several days now.

'Don't stop, don't stop!' Satsuki's head was thrown back, and her hair was spread out. The man's face was buried in her breasts, and he was breathing in gasps.

'Yes, mistress. Yes, mistress,' Okiku heard him mumble. Suddenly she recognised the voice. It was the young servant who had helped her escape from the teahouse. She slipped a hand into her clothes and fingered her moist clit while she admired the thrust of his muscular buttocks. They were smooth and shiny with sweat, and his bag of stones slapped moistly against Satsuki's ass cheeks.

Satsuki suddenly squealed, and her hips ground frenziedly against the boy. 'I'm coming. I'm coming!' she gasped deliriously.

The sight was too much of Okiku. She divested herself rapidly of her brown-stained camouflage suit. Naked, she slipped to the side of the bed. Satsuki caught sight of her over the boy's shoulder. Her eyes widened; then she smiled in welcome. She held the man to her with a hard grip of thighs and arms.

'One moment, dear,' she whispered into his ear. 'Don't move. I don't want you to go off prematurely. There's still much use to be had of you.'

He protested and tried to squirm his way deeper into her, but she slapped his balls lightly with a firm hand and twisted away. Before the bewildered servant knew what had happened, he had been turned on his back by the two women. Okiku spread her legs and gratefully lowered herself onto the warm, waiting prick. He clutched at her, his zest renewed by the short interval. His hands sought shyly for her breasts, and when she encouraged him by bending forward, he squeezed them delightedly. Satsuki crooned beside them and watched while Okiku rose up, then lowered herself forcefully onto the supine man. He met her descent by raising his pelvis.

Okiku rode him unmercifully for a while. Occasionally she bent forward and locked her mouth to his, teasing his tongue and lips. At other times, Satsuki, a poor onlooker, offered her mouth or breast to his available mouth or rubbed her cunt with his hand. She giggled as she came again.

The boy was tiring, Satsuki noticed. She had had him the entire evening, and his upward thrusts were getting more languid. Okiku, well on her way to her own delight, failed to notice, or merely thought there was nothing to be done. Satsuki thought otherwise. She slid her hand under his buttocks and at the right time gave him a sharp pinch. He bounded upward, bringing a gasp from Okiku. At the same time, Satsuki slid a high, hard cushion under his muscular behind.

Okiku seemed to wake up from her trance. She rode in the clouds, the stiff pole her only contact with the earth. Faster and faster she moved, jiggling in every direction, while the youth stretched out beneath her like a captive bow. The sensation overcame her. Her fluids showered down, flooding his prick. He gave a final convulsive shudder, held prisoner by her thighs, then erupted himself. She wriggled her ass forcefully onto his erect pole, mindful of her pleasure, which flooded her with waves of delight.

Her shoulders slumped, and she came down from her high and rolled off him. He lay there helpless for a while until Satsuki helped him roll off the cushion. She shooed him gently out. When the fusuma closed behind him, she lay down beside Okiku and stroked the other girl's cheek and breast.

'I'm glad you came,' she said.

'What were you doing with him?' asked Okiku. 'I thought it was beneath your station to consort with a servant...'

'It would be,' laughed the kuge woman, 'but for my plans. If I am to be a courtesan and court men from all stations, I must get used to men of the simpler classes. Besides, it is a good way to keep him grateful to me. I hope he was satisfactory?' she inquired solicitously.

'Yes, quite,' answered Okiku. She yawned. 'I got what you asked for,' she added, 'but I'm terribly tired, and my arm hurts so.'

'Where is it?'

Okiku waved vaguely towards her pile of clothes on the verandah.

Satsuki, seeing her distress, joined her hands and cried an apology. 'You poor thing! Did you have to fight? Are you wounded?'

'No,' said Okiku. 'I merely strained my arm. And I'm so tired.'

'Let me massage it,' begged Satsuki. She cradled Okiku in her arms and gently rubbed the other girl's shoulder. Okiku's breathing deepened into sleep.

She woke in the early afternoon. Her arm still ached from the exercise of the night before. She was in her own house again. Vaguely she remembered that Lady Gojo-no-Satsuki had ordered a palanquin for her early in the morning, and even given her an appropriate gown, since her ninja's clothing would be highly inappropriate.

Okiku stretched luxuriously on her pallet. She set about making her preparations for the day. The elaborate hairdo took time, as did the choice of robe. In a different part of the house she could hear the

161

maid bustling to and fro, busily going about her tasks. The sounds of the street reached her faintly, the calls of the hawkers reminding her she was hungry.

'Otsu!' she called out. The maid hurried in and bowed.

'We'll have some fish today. Fresh squid if you can get any.' She was sure that squid was one of Jiro's favourite foods, and a wave of self-pity at her grass-widow condition swept over her. Otsu hurried out, and Okiku proceeded with the last chores of her toilet, then went to inspect the garden. The sound of a public announcement from the street caught her ears, but the crier's voice was too muffled for her to get the message.

Otsu returned with her basket.

'Did you get it?'

'No, mistress. But I got some lovely sweet ayu instead.' She showed Okiku the small delicious fish. Okiku gazed at it sadly. An omen, she decided, that Jiro would not be back that day.

'What was the public announcement?' she asked idly.

'Oh, the governor is back. He had been in seclusion because of a ritual pollution, but the dangerous period has passed, and he is back in residence.'

Okiku's heart leaped. Goemon was back! Perhaps action was about to begin, and perhaps he had brought Jiro with him, unlikely as that might be.

'Call a palanquin for me when darkness falls,' she said to the maid. 'I shall be going out.'

Okiku stepped out of the plain wooden palanquin. The bearer held open the mat screening respectfully. Then the two sturdy men hoisted their carrying pole and loped off into the dark, looking for another customer. She crossed the darkened road, crossed a busy marketway, and entered a narrow alley. There was a long whitewashed plaster wall on one side. Set into it inconspicuously was a small door. She scratched at it softly. She waited for a short while, then knocked again. It opened a mere crack, and Okiku made to slip inside, when a large hand dropped onto her shoulder.

She spun around and dropped into a fighting crouch. Jiro grinned at her. He was travel stained and looked weary. She looked at him in mock disgust.

'Phoo! You smell!'

'And I'm also tired and hungry. I passed by the house, but that new maid said you had gone out. I assumed, since you took a palanquin, that you were coming here.' He grinned, enjoying his own perspicacity.

Okiku smiled prettily, glad her man was back. 'Come on; the door is open.' They slipped through the door and it closed behind them. Oko, Rosamund's maid and the only one in the governor's mansion who had an inkling of the double life he led, motioned them to follow her. The way was familiar. It passed through several musty corridors, over a small canal that did double duty as a moat, and into the fastness of the governor's private quarters.

Oko stopped and looked at the pair following her. She coughed delicately.

'It might be preferable to remedy your toilet, Master Miura.'

Jiro scratched his ear and smiled in embarrassment.

163

'You're quite right,' Okiku decided for him. 'Can he have a bath?'

Oko bowed in assent. 'And there are clothes ready for his use. Formal ones.'

They met in a small formal reception room. Matsudaira Konosuke was dressed impeccably. His oiled hair shone, and his rich brocade robe and surcoat contrasted with Miura Jiro's darker costume. Rosamund's blonde hair was piled on her head in an elaborate coiffure, and multicoloured robes peeped, layer under layer, at the neckline. Okiku was dressed more plainly, befitting her rank, but her fewer robes only emphasised the strong, spare lines of her clavicle and throat.

Matsudaira/Goemon looked around him with satisfaction.

'I am glad to be back. I arrived this morning from Osaka with a load of matchlocks and shot. They are scattered about the city, and the only way to stop the rebels is to cut off the head. A merchant of Osaka, Rokuro, is one of the heads of the plot. I can only hope you have found the others.'

Jiro's face was impassive as he bowed slightly and spoke in the air before him. 'Matsudaira Nobutaka, lord of Yoshida. He is another.'

'A distant cousin. Of mine . . . and of the Presence.' Matsudaira Konosuke nodded, and his spine straightened. 'This is serious indeed. Are you certain?'

Jiro dug into his capacious sleeve and produced a small rosette of black slow match.

'Yes,' he said, and laid the slow match on the floor beside him, then slid it forward for Matsudaira's inspection.

'Mizuno-no-kami, a kuge,' added Okiku. She was

pleased with herself and could not help but give a small grin at her success.

Matsudaira raised his eyebrows at her. She reached into her sash, near the almost hidden hilt of her dagger, and withdrew another match, which she handed him silently.

Matsudaira drew a deep breath. 'Something will have to be done,' he said. 'Reports, please.'

Oko, Rosamund's trusted maid, poured tea and then left, to seat herself outside the only entrance. Goemon folded his arms, and his chin dropped to his chest.

'It's a major problem,' he said. 'There are several things we must do. First and foremost is breaking up this plot without alerting anyone. That means we can't challenge, can't create any kind of disturbance...'

'Could we trump up some sort of charge against them and then have them arrested?' Rosamund was sitting less formally than her friends, her legs to her side.

'No,' said Goemon. 'That, too, would attract attention. Besides, what possible charge could arrest a foreigner, a lord, a kuge, and a merchant all together – except treason?'

'Assassinate them,' said Okiku with finality.

'Of course. But how?' retorted Goemon.

'Don't forget we also have to rescue the two novices,' chimed in Jiro. His massive frame was at ease on the flat cushion, and his hands lay flat and relaxed on his knees.

'That's not too easy,' said Goemon. 'Matsudaira is in the Sanjo Inn. It is designed especially for visiting lords, and the plotters are never there together.'

Okiku shrugged. 'It doesn't matter how it's designed. I can penetrate it, and once in, I can let the rest of you –' She broke off, for Goemon was shaking his head violently.

'No, Okiku. You don't understand the problem. The Sanjo Inn was designed to foil attempts by ninja to penetrate it. There are traps and passages and spyholes only the owners and the visiting lords know of. The place is enormous and well stocked, though you'd never know it from the outside. It has more stories than can be seen from the street – the architecture cleverly conceals many features – and there are lots of traps. There's even a No stage there, in case a visiting patron is literarily inclined. We either have to split up, which weakens us, get them together by some ruse, or else hit them one after the other. And I'm afraid that by the time we've hit one, the others will have realised what is going on. We have to think of a way to get them all together, then kill them swiftly and without fuss. Matsudaira hasn't many men there. He doesn't want to call too much attention to himself, and his men are scattered around the city. That's about the only advantage we have.'

'Perhaps we need more people,' said Okiku thoughtfully.

'We cannot share this secret with anyone,' snapped Goemon.

'Not share the secret,' said Okiku placatingly. 'Only use her as bait . . .'

'Her?' asked Jiro. 'Who do you have in mind?'

'It's rather complicated,' said Okiku. 'We've been thinking in circles because we're not thinking humanly.'

'What does that mean?' asked Jiro suspiciously.

Okiku's lovemaking was imaginative, very manipulative of her partners, and sometimes unexpectedly painful. Having grown up to appreciate bluntness, he found her subtlety somewhat upsetting.

'Well,' she smiled, 'let's consider the qualities of each of our opponents and use them to our benefit. Subtlety will get you anywhere, my love.' She patted his crotch familiarly and laughed. Sharp white teeth showed beneath cherry-red lips, and her eyes danced with mischief.

'First' – she counted on her fingers – 'the lesser problems. The merchant Rokuro appears to be fond of very sophisticated delights. From your account, Goemon, I gather he spends much time appreciating the subtler beauties. I gather he has no objection to women, and I have the right woman for him . . . Next, the barbarian. For him we need nothing subtle. Any female figure will do. He'll chase, and you, my love, will remove his head with that too large sword of yours.'

'What makes you think I can beat him in a fair fight?' growled Jiro half-seriously.

'Of course you will. Besides, who said "fair fight"? Kill him, that's all. Then the kuge. I will take care of that dog's head. I have a score to settle, and there'll be no fair fight either. Finally, we can all converge on the Sanjo Inn. I think Rosamund's habit will come in use here. We'll use her as bait. He seems to have a fondness for the clerical. When he sends out his men to grab her, we grab them and disguise ourselves with their hoods – they'd hardly dare kidnap anyone on the streets without them.'

'It sounds too complicated to me –' started Goemon.

'Then come up with a better idea!' she snapped.

'I can't,' he said unhappily, 'and that's the problem. Let's look at it once more. Besides, I will not risk Rosamund. She is in my care, and if something happened, we'd be in worse trouble than otherwise.'

'What do you mean "risk Rosamund"?' the blonde girl demanded. She wagged a finger in his face. 'I will not have you protecting me, or condescending either!'

Slightly irritated, Goemon retorted with some heat, 'I'm keeping you here barely on the right side of the law. I cannot risk you outside!'

'I go outside whenever I will. I'm good at my disguise, and I know how to protect myself as well!' Her eyes flashed dangerously, and Jiro knew Goemon was going to look forward to a difficult evening.

In his most magisterial tones, Goemon answered her, enunciating each word carefully, 'You are not going on with being bait for anyone. I want you live and ready when I come back.'

She swore in Spanish, then in Dutch and English. Jiro, the only one who could understand gutter versions of the latter two languages, winced and wondered where she had picked those expressions up. Her lips thinned, and she subsided. Later Jiro noticed a faint smile playing about her lips. Had it been Okiku who had noticed, Rosamund would have been challenged on the spot, but Jiro's mind did not run on crooked tracks.

They finalised their plans. Okiku would assault Mizuno in his house. She now knew enough about it to plan an ambush there. Later she would return to Satsuki's new dwelling, follow Rokuro when he left, and dispose of him. Jiro would trace the captain to his dwelling. He would challenge the foreigner on some excuse and kill him. They would all then join forces at the Sanjo Inn. Okiku would find them an entry, and they would attack and kill Matsudaira somehow, relying on the small number of his guards and on the element of surprise.

Chapter 10

Satsuki's head was whirling with excitement. This was the first day of her new job, her new life, her newly found profession. She wondered whether she would do well.

She surveyed her new quarters complacently. They would do; they would do indeed. The craftsmen had done a remarkable rush job, she knew. Some more refurbishing would need to be done, but at least on the second floor she could use two large rooms for her work. Both were immaculate and ornamented with the quiet and restrained good taste that was the hallmark of the true nobility.

'Matsuo!' she called out.

'Yes, mistress,' responded the faithful servant from the other side of the shoji.

'Have you introduced yourself to the shops in the neighbourhood? Are we assured of ready supplies?'

'Yes, mistress. And there are several discreet requests for employment.'

'We will consider them in due time,' she answered in satisfaction. She had brought two of her maids with her from the kuge quarter. She wandered over to the window in the innermost room, which would serve as her main working area. The bedding was of course hidden discreetly in the closets, and the pure tatami, still tinged with the green of freshness, smelled of the countryside. She wandered over to the window and looked out over grey tiled roofs to the wooden slopes of Higashiyama, whose peak was softened by the afternoon sun.

Below her she heard the sounds of an arriving guest. Matsuo's discreet voice broke into her reverie. 'Mistress, Lady Miura is here.'

'Bring her here, please.' She hastily arrayed herself on the tatami, casting a critical eye on her multilayered brocade robes. Her face reflected back at her from a small mirror. She studied it for a brief moment. A tiny, solemn white mask peered back at her. Her lips were carmine, the faint smudges of her painted eyebrows high on a smooth forehead. The lines of her face flowed smoothly as befitted an aristocrat of Miyako. Above her face, her hair was piled up in a fanciful hairdo. She had looked at commoner women and had decided to imitate their style but in her own way. Her hairdo was a perfection of coiling smooth piles of hair, held in place by fine gold pins.

Okiku entered the room, knelt and bowed in greeting.

Satsuki bowed deeply back. 'You are welcome,' she said formally. 'Please come in.'

Okiku looked at her and gasped. 'But you are beautiful!' she blurted.

Satsuki kept her face impassive for a long breath,

171

then burst out in a giggle. 'It is rather effective, isn't it? I'm so glad you like it.'

'It will create a sensation. I'm almost afraid to introduce my men to you.'

Satsuki answered with a twinkle, 'You know I'll always give them back.'

They laughed, and Okiku came closer to sit before her friend.

'Have you any propositions from customers yet?' she asked confidentially.

'No,' answered the former kuge, 'but I'm sure there will be some soon.'

Not looking at her friend, Okiku murmured, 'I might have someone for you, but . . . but it's a difficult thing to ask . . .'

Satsuki said nothing, merely waited for Okiku to find the words.

'You have an idea what I do. I do it for a very important personage.' Satsuki nodded at Okiku's fumbling words. 'There is a certain man we are interested in. I . . . have to deal with him . . . I won't do it here, of course, but I need to have him delayed while I engage in something else. He is here in the quarter. Do you think you could do it?'

'Of course I can do it, but what kind of a person is this? I can hardly expect to start with someone of the lowest class.'

'He is a rich merchant from Osaka. A former samurai, I believe. He purveys goods to the Hall.'

'Ah, then he must be a refined man. I'd be delighted to accept him. Could you point him out to Matsuo? We can work out some sort of approach.'

'Remember though, dear, that he is a very dangerous man. You must keep him happy without any indication of duplicity.'

Satsuki, involved in herself, had not noticed how tense Okiku was. Suddenly her manner came into focus, as did her manner of dress. Okiku wore a simply patterned spring robe, but under it Satsuki could see the outline of other clothes. And when Okiku moved her hand she was careful to conceal her forearms. Looking carefully, Satsuki fancied she could see the sleeve of the woven body armour ninja wore to work.

'What exactly is going to happen to this customer?' she asked cautiously.

It was Okiku's turn to be bland. 'I imagine he will cease from purveying goods to the All under Heaven . . . and to others.'

Not quite understanding but ready to trust her friend and, above all, ready for all intrigue and all twists and turns of her new and exciting career, Satsuki smiled in acquiescence.

'I shall leave with nightfall,' Okiku said as she rose and peered idly through the vertical bars of the window that fronted the street. Something caught her eye, and she peered down intently, then called to her friend.

'That is luck. Satsuki, dear, come here a moment. Here is the man we want, down in the street.'

Satsuki peered into the street beside her. A man in late middle age was strolling down the narrow road, casually glancing at the discreet entrances to the few local shops and teahouses. He was powerfully built, with a commanding presence and greying hair. His middle bulged a bit with advancing years, but he had an indefinable air of self-assurance that came from a life of wealth and giving orders.

'If you send Matsuo after him quickly, he may be able to make an approach to him, and then we could

173

get him here. Or you yourself could go . . .'

Satsuki raise an eyebrow regally. 'There is no need for that. He will come.' She had noticed that the man was also looking casually at the second storey of the buildings he passed, hoping, no doubt, as all gallants did, to catch a glance of the inner occupants. She motioned Okiku peremptorily away and peered down through the bars into the street. Her face betrayed no emotion, but inside she boiled with anticipation. This was the life of real passion and intrigue for which she had left the stale and over-proper kuge quarter.

The tensions of the past few days and the time still left to wait were affecting Rokuro's nerves. He had taken this walk, eastward and away from the scenes of future action, to calm his anticipation. It was always thus for him before desperate action. It had been thus at Sekigahara, where his side had lost the day, and at other battles, where he had been on the winning side. Now he walked on the eve of his greatest battle.

He glanced casually into the semihidden entrances to businesses. Unlike merchants in lusty, brawling, businesslike Osaka, where each merchant strove to outdo the others, those of Miyako seemed to prefer hiding their businesses away from the light. In some ways he preferred their refined way of business, though it always annoyed him that it was almost impossible to find a public eating place in Miyako. Osaka men were known trenchermen, the best cooks in the land, and were contemptuous of all others.

There were plenty of discreet, private dining houses, some of which would welcome him, but he was not hungry yet. So he strolled, occasionally casting glances at the second storey of buildings. The Gion was sparsely settled, though entertainment and dining places were springing up, since it was on the way to the eastern mountain temples such as Kiyomizu, with its famed trestle construction.

A flash of white attracted his eye, and he peered discreetly upwards. Vertical, brown wooden bars obscured his view, but he was struck by the sight of the most perfect face he had ever seen. Like a No mask come to life, the pale white face seemed to float in the window, remote, uncaring, desirable.

Rokuro moistened his lips and considered. There was still plenty of time. He was not often in Miyako, and the bewitching face of the woman in the window tugged at his mind. He cast another look upwards. The vertical wooden bars gave him a distorted view of her face, but its pale stillness burned into the recesses of his mind.

There was a teahouse in the corner, modestly advertising itself, as all such establishments did in Miyako, by nothing more than a blue curtain across a blank door. He entered and was offered tea and the tiny, flower-shaped sugar cakes that are the speciality of Miyako. He asked for good notepaper, and the proprietor, unasked but used to the needs of his refined customers, brought a wisteria branch with it.

Rokuro hastily wrote some lines in a painfully elegant script. He folded the paper and tied it to the branch.

He called a waiter over. 'There is a house down the lane. Please convey this letter there. I will await a reply.'

The waiter bowed and departed. Rokuro sipped at his tea nervously. A new and refined entertainer would be a fine way to restore his equanimity. Tomorrow their futures would be sealed. If the kuge's planning was right, they would at last restore the glory of the imperial house, and the upstart Tokugawa would be swept from the earth. He clapped his hands thrice for luck and bowed towards the god shelf he saw on the wall near the ceiling.

The waiter returned. 'Master, the letter was received by a young man. He gave me this.' The waiter handed Rokuro an intricately folded bamboo leaf. Inside, tied with a pair of pine needles, was a single tiny plum. Rokuro smiled at the signs of felicity and left.

He found a public bath and bathed carefully. It was too late to return to the inn he was staying at, near the Heian shrine, but he knew a clothing shop nearby. The proprietor, an old acquaintance, happily sold him a new outfit. As was only proper for his station, a cotton overrobe went over a silk lining.

'A woman?' asked the shopkeeper, raising his little finger.

Rokuro smiled in acknowledgment.

'The Gion quarter is becoming rather popular for that sort of thing. On the way to the temples on the mountainside but a bit out of the way. If you really want to impress her, I have something special.' He held out a silk loincloth.

Rokuro laughed. 'How will I let people know? After all, one wears silk not just for comfort . . .'

The other laughed with him. 'As for her, she'll indubitably see it anyway. As for others, you'll need a fire . . .'

'A fire?'

'Yes, the midsummer dancing ones. You know, young men jump over them. You could feign drunkenness, then ask with a surprised air, "Hm, I seem to smell silk burning. Must be my underclothes!"' The two merchants laughed.

He left fully equipped, and as dark was coming, he proceeded back to the Gion. A discreet lamp lit the entrance to the house. He knocked lightly at the door, and it opened immediately. A young man was facing him. Without a word he was conveyed to a waiting room furnished with great simplicity. Only a red rose in a simple flower arrangement contrasted to the plain clay walls, golden tatami mats, and clean woodwork. He took out a small box he had packed in his sleeve. It was wrapped in a purple kerchief and was heavier than such a box should be. He placed it gently on the mat beside him.

From the paper-glazed shoji doors before him came the faint sounds of a biwa lute played very softly in the court manner. Two maids entered, both elderly, and knelt by either side of the sliding doors. His heart started pounding in his chest. They drew the sliding doors back, and there was the white-faced woman.

Her hair was piled on her head in an elaborate hairdo. She was dressed in multiple flowing robes that seemed like modifications of the court dress he had seen on scrolls or on the few kuge women he had met. She bowed deeply to him and said in a high-pitched, refined voice with a strong, aristocratic slur, 'Welcome. Please come in and make yourself comfortable.'

He bowed in return and muttered a polite refusal. She urged him in again, and he aquiesced. There was another exchange of courtesies when she urged him to sit on a cushion.

At last he was comfortable. He sat formally on his knees and examined her at length. Idly she stroked the strings of the lute. She knew that her makeup, hair, and clothes were perfect. The collar of her gowns showed just enough of her neck to be titillating, but not too much.

She played several small airs and sang quietly. He applauded gracefully and condescended to have a cup of tea, served by her own hands though prepared by one of the maids.

He told her somewhat of his business, and noted with approval the respectful nod of her head when he mentioned that he dealt with the Honourable Hall. She asked him if he were not tired, and he denied it, though noting that the voyage from Osaka as a lengthy one. She called in one of her maids, who played a flute while she moved through a stately court dance. She bowed at the fusuma at the far side of the room. His pulses leaped. Several candles lit the room, casting a beautiful glow. The gold and brown of the tatami and woodwork served as perfect foil for the dark red of her robe and the pale white of her face floating above it. His passion roused to a furious pitch, he floated unnoticing out of his seat. She turned sideways and opened the fusuma. A wide pallet was ready in the other room, which also contained a small brazier and a smoking mosquito-incense coil. He passed within.

She knelt beside him and loosened his sash, then ran her hands delicately up his legs, across his silk loin cloth, which was bulging with the treasure within, and on to his belly. He idly traced the line of her robe, mentally counting the layers within.

'Your muscles are all tense. I believe I should do something about that.' It pleased her that he had taken the trouble to have a bath before coming to her. It showed his refinement. He looked long at her face, then rolled over onto his belly.

Starting from his calves, she stroked and rubbed the length of his limbs. Sensations of growing languorous pleasure slid up his legs and joined at the crotch. A hard rod dug into the mattress beneath him, and his hips began to twitch. She untied and removed his sash and rolled his robe up to his shoulders. Calling softly, she invited one of her maids in. The diminutive woman's weight pressed on his back as she walked back and forth on him, her toes digging into his sore muscles. The maid stepped off and left the room, and the mistress's smooth hands took over.

There was a whisper of cloth, and he knew she had loosened her own robes. She straddled him and continued the massage. Her cunt came into contact with his hard buttocks, and she slid to and fro above him, her juices lubricating his skin. She used the same moisture as an aid to her hands on his back.

He started groaning uncontrollably. His cock swelled to incredible proportions, and he feared he would poke a hole through the pallet beneath him. She rolled him over on his back and straddled him. Her hands probed at his muscles, loosening the tension in most places, concentrating it in one spot.

He vaguely noticed that she was still dressed in her robes, though her wide sash was gone. The colourful layers contrasted precisely with one another, in perfect harmony with her white skin. She removed his silk loincloth, letting the material slide sensuously over his erect cock. Then she rose slightly, and the black triangle at the junction of her thighs engulfed him.

He almost howled in relief as the soft, moist folds of her tight cunt enveloped the tip of his cock. She let her weight down slowly until she was nestled on his hips and belly. Her hands did not cease from massaging his skin and muscles.

Now she swayed back and forth, squeezing pleasure from every fraction of the length of his pole. With very slight movements she built his passion gradually until his tension grew too much for him to bear. His face contorted, and his head moved involuntarily from side to side. She leaned forward to allow him to squeeze her and suck her breasts, which he did with the air of a drowning man catching at a float. Her hands continued their movements, her hips their gentle undulations.

He was practically sobbing now, her precise control having brought him to a point he had never achieved before with any woman. With a convulsive leap he tried to stab her to her depths. Knowing what was to come, she set her feet firmly beside him, then constricted her muscles as much as she could.

He exploded inside her uncontrollably. His hips arched, and a wordless howl came from between his clenched teeth. He shook in frenzy while she rode him imperturbably. Her impassive white face looked down, spicing his pleasure.

When he had recovered somewhat she fed him bitter summer oranges for his refreshment, peeling each fruit in a perfect spiral, then opening the tough skin of each segment, not with a knife, but with her own perfect teeth. She left him then for a while. An illustrated scroll of court dances kept him entertained.

She returned newly dressed, her hairdo subtly rearranged. She sang again, a sprightly marching tune, then fed him a small meal of tiny pounded rice cake in sweet soup, salted seaweed, and refreshing bitter tea.

Unlike her previous appearance, her mood in direct contrast was coy, even girlish. She giggled often, tickled and teased him, slid her hands suggestively about his body under his robe. Throughout he was conscious of the stylised poses and gestures she made as she imitated with elegant perfection the wiles of a teenage girlish lover. Entranced, he felt his member rising again at her bidding.

'We must try it naked. I'm so hot!' she said plaintively.

Rapidly they stripped. His wiry body, only beginning to show the changes of age, was a brown contrast to the whiteness of her skin. She paused for a moment to allow him to admire her. Her tiny waist was bound by pleasantly wide thighs. Her legs were smooth, her belly a gentle dome broken only by the shadow of her navel. Beneath lay the mysterious cavern of her sex, obscured by a perfect black triangle. Her shoulders and neck were lightly powdered, making that area beautifully sensuous.

Languidly she knelt and turned her back, then peeked at him over her shoulder. 'As you please, master,' she said, and bowed to the floor.

He admired the curve of her backside for a moment. The channel between her half moons was slightly darker, and the lower beard showed the purse of her cunt to advantage. His lust raged at the sight. Hurriedly he covered her with his body. His rounded belly smacked solidly onto the roundness of her ass. He leaned forward and grasped her breasts while his long tongue lapped sensuously at her back, shoulders, and neck. The taste of her sweat mingled with the flavour of the rice powder she had used to whiten her shoulders, aroused indescribably

181

pleasurable feelings. He shuttled back and forth into her, slowly increasing the speed of his movements. The tip of his cock probed her very depths, and from the uncontrolled shivering of her hips, he knew that at last she was moving with him towards a climax.

He increased the tempo of his pistoning, and at the same time his tongue lapped quicker and quicker at her exquisite skin. His hands moulded her smooth, pale breasts almost without his willing them. Their tension grew to a peak, and her cunt constricted, clipping the tip of his pole. He gave one last shove and buried himself to the hairs in her. Holding this pose he spurted gobs of liquid into her raging insides.

While the ripples of pleasure were shaking her insides to a jelly, Satsuki was worried. Okiku was late, very late. It was clear what she wanted this merchant for. She had as much as admitted that she was going to kill him. But if she did not arrive soon, the man would leave. This mysterious appointment of his would take him away. A thought crossed her mind. Perhaps there was a way out. Okiku was her friend, and she must be helped. Perhaps there was a way of keeping him here or, even better...

Chapter 11

Lord Matsudaira Nobutaka of Yoshida was well pleased with himself. His pleasure found expression in the thin smile that occasionally curved his lips, in a greater restlessness of manner, and in greater attention to his own entertainments.

He was dressed in the full robes of the warrior from the play *Star Isle*. Stiff gold-coloured silk clothes covered his body, and his face, covered with the mask of a fierce warrior, was contorted in a grimace of effort. The other actors wore nothing but their masks. Two wore women's faces. Smooth porcelain like skin, rounded faces, eyes closed to mere slits, eyebrows high on a swelling smooth forehead. Another two wore the fierce faces of demons of jealousy: bulging gilt eyeballs peering out from beneath heavy brows, wide noses overshadowing fanged mouths, horned brows.

The arrangement was unconventional, Matsudaira knew. There should be three, not five, main characters, and the others were not doing their part. Well, they would learn – if they survived.

The stage was a small square slightly raised. The left wing was an open passageway where the actors could pose. The sole prop was a small pine tree, and another was painted as backdrop. He paced through the gestures, mouthing the sonorous poetry with feeling. The other actors stood in their assigned places, not moving.

He detected a slight tremor in the naked limbs of one of the demons. His fan slashed down, raising a welt on the perfect thigh. He placed his foot deliberately on the boards, thumping the stage in counterpoint to the blow.

He finished his delivery and stood watching his fellow actors. They were still in their assigned places. Good. They would make a troupe yet – a private one, of course. And their being two sets of twins had peculiar technical interest: disappearances and appearances on stage could be easily managed, with or without masks.

He took two paces back and watched the tableau. One woman-masked twin was kneeling near the pine. Her cone-shaped breasts, tipped with black nipples, stood out proudly, casting a shadow down her lean belly to the mossy grove between her thighs. He turned his head. Her mirror image was standing stiffly at the entrance to the stage. As he had taught her, her hands were held well away from her body, and her feet were flat on the boards.

A demon was kneeling with her back to the backdrop. Matsudaira admired the contrast between the fierce scowling face and the smooth roundness of the hips and breasts. Rounded areolas and nipples stared at him in mute counterpoint to the glowing golden eyeballs above.

Finally, the demon came near him. She still stood as posed, right arm raised threateningly in a curve over her head, left heel across her body as if holding a sleeve away from a touch. Her heavy hips and stocky legs emphasised the charm of the mossy beard that hung below her belly. Through the eyeholes of his mask he could barely see the sweet lips hanging between her legs. Her right breast was tautly visible, held up by the movement of her arm. Seeing the mask gaze at her, she trembled again. He stepped around and behind her, moving from the hips, his steps delicate but solidly planted. The feel of the boards reacting against his tread transmitted itself to his skull and the rest of him.

'Bend!' he said almost inaudibly. She stifled a sob and did as she was told. The curve of her back excited him. He ran the fan up the length of the crack, then down it. At the same time his other hand freed his tumescent member from the loose hakama trousers he wore. He smashed the long fleshy pole down on her buttocks. Experience by now with his whims, the ex-novice did not move. He bent and forced it between her legs, the top of his shaft caressing but not entering the smooth lips. He found the pose unsatisfactory and smacked her buttocks with the fan again.

'Resume your pose,' he ordered her, then circled before her. He tucked the fan in his waistband and pinched each nipple between finger and thumb. The mask returned a fierce gaze. He peered into the demon's scowl, feeling the emotion the mask projected, feeling awed and victorious at once. Beneath the mask, the boy twisted, pale, almost translucent, trembled at his touch. His hands

185

gripped her hips, fingers digging into the softness of her buttocks, and he bent slightly at the knees until the tip of his raging cock beat at the V of her legs. Without aiming, he thrust upwards. His cock hit painfully against her pubic bone and slid up the length of her lower belly. He drew back and tried again, only to miss. The stiff brocade of his robes rubbed painfully against the girl's skin, and the power of his fingers added bruises to those that already marred her ass. He slammed forward once again, then again, leaving trails of slickness and reddened skin. At last she forced herself to accommodate him. She opened her legs and managed to aim his long lance up her narrow channel. The relief for both of them was immediate. The prodding of his cock against her little button had stimulated feelings she had tried to repress. She sighed behind the mask, peering into the fierce warrior's face, as the long, warm pole reached its destination.

His motions grew frenzied now. She gasped at the pain and the pleasure of it. She tried to control her hands. Involuntarily they sought to clutch at the muscular body beneath the brocade. She knew he would beat her if she did hold him, and she refrained. Muted gasps came from her mouth. Her tongue peeped out from between her fangs. He pushed deeper into her without withdrawing. Tremors reached from the depths of her cervix along the tissues of her narrow tube. Her cunt constricted and twitched, and a flood of moisture inundated his inflamed cock as she came. Involuntarily she ground her pelvis into him and rubbed her inflamed nipples against his rough chest. Her spasms slowed as her coming shuddered to a stop.

He withdrew from her. She was about to collapse, when his fan caught her beneath the chin.

'I gave you no permission to move!' he said. 'Resume your pose.' She did so and felt her juices run sliding down her legs. Her mask face stared in anger at his back.

Matsudaira walked across the stage to One, who was kneeling by the pine. His tread was deliberate, as befitted a No actor. Each foot came down precisely, and the next step followed after all movement of the previous step had ended. He posed before the calm woman's face, his prick glistening as it swung before the mask. He squatted before her and pinched both breasts together, then shoved his cock between the two beautiful mounds.

His cock was a red-hot spear. The tip was wet from its previous use and from the sweat that ran down the girl's chest and pooled between her breasts. He let go of her tits and they bounced back to their natural shape. She watched him go without a quiver, too used to his moods and violence even to think of demanding the satisfaction that her body craved. In any case, she knew, she and her sister would soon have their fill of those haughty nuns, now dressed as very unusual demons. She watched curiously as her master stumped across the stage. He moved with the care of an actor. Feet were placed precisely. The tension in the stiffly held torso expressed precisely the rising lust and male strength of him as he moved. Her sister stood like a statue, awaiting his coming. The kneeling one could imagine the sight from the front, the severe warrior face looming closer, the naked sword peering out from the folds of the trousers.

At last Matsudaira reached her. She made a proper

187

gesture of fear, right hand rising in an arc, hand open before her face, timed perfectly to meet his advance. He moved his hands to the side, then seized her shoulders and bore her to the floor, each measure a balanced act in itself. Without pausing he rammed his stiff cock into her to the hilt. Stiff brocade scratched the sensitive inner skin of her thighs, and she sighed voluptuously as she stared, hypnotised, at the fierce, re-painted wooden features above her. Behind the features, she knew, were the eyes and mind of her lover. She locked her legs strongly behind his ass, luxuriating in the scratchiness of the material along her legs. He pushed in as far as possible, then slowly pulled the length of his cock out again.

The two masks communicated in silence and immobility as the bodies that carried them writhed on the boards. His gestures became harder, more hurried. He ground his hips into her softness, evoking a light cry of pain, which only caused him to force himself in deeper. He lifted his entire weight so that it rested on her pubic bone and rocked himself back and forth. She felt herself beginning to climax from the intensity of the feeling and her love. Her hands clutched at his broad back as he rocked back and forth into her. His movements became savage, and he drove stiff fingers into her straining buttocks, then ground his hips in a circular motion into the bowl of her belly.

Suddenly he stiffened, his entire weight resting like a bow on the single point of her cunt. Stream after stream of thick cream gushed from his prick and inundated her insides, washing away the pain and bringing down her own pleasure in turn. Her eyes glazed as her peak ripped through her. She wished she could swallow him whole, entire, and she urged him forward with hip and fingers.

He withdrew from her slowly. His cock, she noted regretfully, was still hard. As the warrior mask receded from her, she smiled inside her own mask. He had many women and would have more, but he was hers and her sister's in ways that others did not have.

Erect, the front of his trousers smeared with his own and the girl's emissions, Matsudaira approached the kneeling demon. The demon shuddered in fear at the warrior's commanding approach.

'Stroke me properly,' the warrior commanded. He looked distinterestedly at the pine tree before him as the demon's hands reached out and fumbled uncertainly at his juice-covered stick. The monster erection hardened again and rose to its full glory. The demon's soft hands moulded the length of the shaft, eyeing the single hole at the tip in horrified fascination. Without a word the warrior pulled his sword away.

'Bow down before me!'

The demon knelt in fear. The warrior stepped around and admired the smooth, moonlike ass, the dark split between the two mounds, and the tiny show of hairs that almost brushed the floor. The blood pounded in the warrior's temples as he knelt behind the subservient demon. He stuck his fingers into the smooth hips before him. His entire body trembled a moment before the instant of his triumph; then, with a final cry, he stabbed his lance up into the juncture of the demon's thighs.

There was no pause before the gush of sperm travelled from his heated balls up the channel of his prick. Wave after wave of juice spurted out, inundating her channel and overflowing to the ground. She grunted in surprise as the full weight of the man's body collapsed on her. Her own insides twitched. The thrust had not been entirely unpleasant, and she braced herself for more, which might bring her own hoped-for pleasure. But the weight on her back did not move. Even the punishing fingers, which usually explored every nook and cranny of her, did nothing more than hold on to her hips painfully. All five waited in a frozen tableau for a long moment.

Matsudaira rolled off the girl and rose to his feet. Without a word he turned and walked off into the gloom of the hall. The four girls rose to their feet, the novices numb, the twins, Lady One and Lady Two, with alacrity and purpose. They shed their masks and replaced them in cedar-wood boxes.

'Light the candles. It's too gloomy in here,' ordered Two.

The novice closest to her, Saiho, looked about for her robe.

'What are you doing?' asked Two furiously.

'Looking for my robe . . .' the girl's voice trailed off.

'You won't need it for a while,' Lady One giggled from the other side of the stage. 'I haven't had enough. Have you?' she asked her sister.

'Light those extra candles and come here.'

Chie, the other novice, obeyed. Her thighs were still dripping, and she walked with them joined together to avoid dripping on the floor.

'Let me see that,' commanded One imperiously. Chie came to a stop, and One inserted a hand between her legs. She stroked the slit for a moment. Unwillingly, Chie's hips jerked in response, and her insides quivered. One laughed. 'First me; then we'll

190

see about you.'

One and Two had the other two twins lie on the floor. They squatted over the obedient mouths and began to rock themselves back and forth. Knowing their mistresses' desires, Chie and Saiho stretched out their tongues into the deep warm hollows that almost suffocated them. Their tongues darted and swooped in the way they had been taught by the prioress of Dosojin-ji. First they stuck their oral digits deep into the waiting caverns. Then they commenced licking the length of the inner lips, pausing now and again to suck in a portion of the fleshy lips.

At last they reached the nubbin at the front of each exquisite purse. They sucked in the tiny fingers of flesh, nibbling with their teeth at the outside fleshy layer, careful to avoid biting too hard. They licked back again, and the rocking motion of their mistresses speeded up. Though they could not hear it, above them One and Two were panting audibly.

Unable to bear the pleasure passively any longer, One stuck her fingers between her legs and roughly massaged her clit, rubbing fingers through the silky growth of hair between her legs and pinching the lips together over the sensitive button. She came with a hiss like a kettle, ramming her hips down onto Chie's hapless lips, almost suffocating her in her own pleasure.

As Two felt her own pleasure approach, she suddenly leaned over and smelled appreciatively between Saiho's legs. The wonderful aromatic smell of the fresh young cunt was overlaid by the headier musk of a male. She spread the girl's thighs apart with strong, rough hands and covered the exposed lips with her own mouth, sucking in the entire fleshy flower. Her teeth scraped lightly against Saiho's clit as her tongue plumbed the depths of Saiho's channel. Her own cunt was lapped from top to bottom with rapid flicks as Saiho's approaching climax, unexpected as it was quick, threw her into a frenzy.

They came together in a swirl of clenching limbs. Each girl's limbs clenched around the other's head. They twitched and shuddered as if they were one double-backed, headless beast. The tempo of their licking and sucking died down at last, and Two rolled off her victim. Saiho's face was wet, and she wore a puzzled look on her face. This was the first time either of the twins had voluntarily done anything for her.

Silently the two novices rose and bowed. They began cleaning the room as One and Two left, gathering their clothing as they walked.

'We must get out of here,' Saiho whispered as they worked. She was well aware the inn was full of listening posts, and there was no way of checking whether they were overheard.

'How?' asked Chie succinctly.

'Later. Across the roof. We can climb out through the tiny window in the gable. I saw one of the bodyguards check it today, but it was poorly secured. It overlooks an eave that ends near the road. We must try, we must –' She was near hysterics.

'Shh!' said her twin, who could think of no objection. They both knew they were alive only at the whim of Matsudaira, and he was mad enough to kill them at any time. 'Very well. Later, then.'

Chapter 12

'Onna, come here!'

The servant girl, used to such peremptory summonses, knelt and bowed before her master. He studied her carefully. Her hair was relatively short, and the plain cotton robe she wore hid a chunky but pleasing figure. She had the smooth, round moon face found among the commoners in Miyako, the result of centuries of interbreeding with the aristocracy.

He was unusually tense, a feeling he did not like and was not used to. He wished Satsuki were here to relieve his tension, but if she had been, she would have become aware of his plans too. This was the day, he thought triumphantly, while the servant girl knelt before him. This miserable villa would be traded for a magnificent palace when he took his rightful place. The samurai might think he would rule, but only one such as Mizuno-no-kami, with his impeccable pedigree and breeding, could really sit at the apex, right under the All under Heaven, ruling in his name as great minister. He smiled savagely, unaware that his hands had turned to claws. The tiny lacquered wooden bowl he held in his hands broke with a snapping sound.

The sound brought him out of his reverie. 'More sake,' he ordered.

She poured the drink into the old-fashioned flat cup and handed it to him with both hands extended. He drank and held out the cup again. She filled and offered it, and he drank half. Catching sight of her patient face behind the rim of the cup, he remembered the evening almost a year ago when he had taken her maidenhead. She had been unwilling at first, but like most women in his presence, she had soon given in. Different from kuge women, he'd decided, somewhat like eating millet gruel after becoming used to a diet of fine polished white rice: not a bad change if not indulged in too often.

He handed her the cup. 'Drink!' he commanded.

She giggled and turned her face away in an attempt at refusal. 'Drink!' he ordered. She covered the cup with both plump palms and drank the remainder. He filled it for her again, and she drank. Her cheeks flushed and the look in her eye brightened. She knew what was to come. He reached for her and pulled her to him.

She spread her legs willingly as he raised the skirts of her robe. They were nice legs, he decided. Rather browner than he liked, less refined, but nicely shaped. He knelt between her legs and allowed her to loosen the tapes that tied his loose trousers. His neatly manicured hands with their long nails opened the bosom of her dress.

She had well-developed breasts, now lying against

194

her chest. Dark nipples with large brown areolas winked back at him. He fondled them, not too gently, and she smiled shyly. He stroked lower; then his hand went behind her back to loosen her sash. He stroked her full ass. It was well muscled, and her skin quivered at his touch. He laid his palms flat on her belly, the thumbs just barely tracing the hairs that rose from between her thighs. The heart-shaped patch of mossy growth tickled the tips of his thumbs as he slid his hands lower. Between his two thumbs he pinched the little hood that hid her tiny clitoral bud. She moaned at the expected touch, and her eyes closed.

He cupped the entire mound of her pussy with his palm and slid his middle finger into the juicy cavity. Her hips wiggled as she sought to swallow the intruder with her nether mouth. His other hand spread her thighs wider, and he leaned forward, resting his torso's weight on one hand. The tip of his cock knocked against the back of his hand. He removed his hand and sought for the entry with his ready manroot. The rubbery tip banged against quivering thighs, then against the softness of the clitoris. She moaned again and moved, attempting to trap him. He banged his cock several times against the forest between her thighs, barely missing the target each time, being in no great hurry. She smiled slightly, her lids barely opened, examining his long pale face.

At last he relented. The length of his prick sank slowly and without hindrance into her hungry orifice. He let his entire weight press onto her until their hairs meshed. He lay there for a while, nibbling delicately at her tits, then at the smooth skin near her collarbone. Her breathing slowed for a while, then gradually quickened. Her hands slipped over his back, then drew down to his buttocks to urge him on. He withdrew even more slowly than he had come in, then stabbed at her again. She raised her pelvis to meet him. Again and again he withdrew, then fell down on her soft belly and softer cunt. The speed of his movements picked up. She urged him forward with her hands on his straining buttocks.

Without his noticing, his breathing became quicker and louder. Her moans increased each time a twist of their bodies brought heightened sensitivity to some particularly sensitive spot. Now his hands started clutching almost uncontrollably at her body. He felt as if his eyes were glazing. She urged him on with her hands, pulling him into her. His wild thrusts brought a wilder response from her. Her hips leaped into the air, as if she were trying to buck off the weight she really wanted. His ramming body met the rhythm of her leaps, and a slapping sound, gradually increasing in tempo, came from the slickly sweaty bellies as they smacked together.

A long-drawn-out cry, muffled in the skin of her shoulder, came from him as his juice spurted from his tense balls. Spasm after spasm laced through the length of his cock, inundating her warm and slick insides. His cock became almost painfully sensitive, and his body wriggled in her soft body like a speared fish. He suddenly felt a clipping sensation as her climax joined his. She looked at his contorted face and sighed happily, closing her eyes as her pleasure shivered down her insides.

They lay quietly for a while, his shrinking member still in her. At last he rolled off and lay on his back. She smiled at him over her naked shoulder. With a quick movement she slipped her robe up onto her shoulder, then retied her sash. He sat up and rearranged his trousers. She knelt before him to pour some more rice wine, but he stopped her with a gesture.

'Some tea would be better. Please have it brought.'

She bobbed a bow and turned to go. As she slid the shoji shut behind her, Mizuno thought he heard a faint sound from the ceiling beams overhead. The faintest of sounds repeated as she shuffled off down the polished wooden boards of the corridor. He put a hand to his head to readjust the black gauze eboshi hat.

With a sudden movement the thin knife he had withdrawn from his eboshi flipped towards the tiny opening where a ceiling panel had been slightly moved. The panel slammed shut. With one step he rose and took down the ancient polearm hanging over the sliding door. He stabbed up through the ceiling at the slight sounds of feet above the ceiling.

Suspecting what was to come, Okiku leaped onto a cross beam under the roof. The thrown dirk had come uncomfortably close. Had she not slammed down the panel, it would have penetrated her eye. A thick curved blade stabbed up once, then again through the ceiling panels. Well, she thought, there was nothing for it but to get down and do the job. Mizuno didn't seem to be calling for help, and if she hurried, he would soon be dead.

She dipped a hand into the small pouch at her side. The rat squeaked indignantly at her. She released the animal on the ceiling panel, then ran lightly along the beam away from the animal. The blade appeared again, distracted by the rat. Swiftly she raised a panel and dropped through it without a sound. Mizuno's profile was to her, but it was the

197

sudden weight on the tatami that alerted him. Her sword cut missed him by inches as he turned to face her. His halberd, massive bladed, whistled at her head in response. She ducked and moved forward, stabbing with her straight blade over her crooked elbow at his exposed throat. His own blade saved him. She twisted to follow its movement as it swept at her feet and felt a sharp stab of pain over her eyebrow. She leaped lightly back and crouched facing him.

'You were the one who was here before,' he said while she felt her brow. A thin metal needle was stuck into the skin. Had it hit the eye, she would have lost much of her vision and her fighting will to boot. She plucked the needle out as he spun the halberd in an intricate rhythm and advanced on her. She could see no break in his defence and was forced to retreat until her back was to a shoji door. She pushed hard with her back, and the shoji fell out. She faked a retreat, then sprang forward, rolling horizontally at his legs.

He tripped over her and rolled to the ground but was on his feet as quickly as she. They faced one another, panting heavily. He stalked her, the sweep of his antique heavy halberd a blur, sometimes high, sometimes low. She circled cautiously. Now she found herself back in the passageway. He charged, expecting to pin her against the outer shutters of the house. She leapt high, trying to reach an overhead beam, remembering as she leapt the trap that had caught her before.

Her caution was her saving. She barely touched the top of the beam with her fingertips. One finger was cut badly by the steel blades embedded there. Using her precarious grip and swinging her body in desperation, she swung over his surprised head to the next beam she saw was free. Her foot knocked his tall hat from his head, confusing him for the necessary second. She got a grip on the beam. With a crack it fell neatly into two sawed halves. Another trap. She fell with the beam on top of her. It missed her head, but bruised her tired shoulder. This time, too, she knew, she had been defeated. Launching herself through the air she smashed at the wooden shutters. Held only by shallow grooves, they fell outward. She rolled through the opening as the halberd struck again at her. She ran for the wall, dropping tiny steel caltrops behind her. They were long enough to stop even a woven straw sandal.

Mizuno watched the ninja scale the wall and disappear in the dark. With an effort he tried to calm his breathing. It was the same assassin, he was sure now. He still did not know how the assassin had got away the first time, but the skill she displayed was a partial explanation. He considered calling his servants. None of them were reliable enough to be in the plot. In some obscure fashion he was sure the assassin's appearance was related to their moves tonight. He would have to inform Lord Matsudaira, and quickly. They would have to move up the timing. He turned to dress himself, then hurried through the night, a sword hanging at his side, to the Sanjo Inn.

Captain Agostinho DaSilva was drunk and happy. He had drunk a powerful, newly made sake. He had also rid himself of the dangerous load of matchlocks that Rokuro had forced him to carry to Miyako. He did not care for this city. It was too staid, and there was no entertainment quarter he could discern. He had had no audience with the emperor of the Japans. A courtier with painted face and a tall black hat had seen him and his gifts, then dismissed him in a languid tone. The ubiquitous smiling faces were tiresome. And they had not understood his demand for a woman.

Rokuro was nowhere to be seen. He had disappeared on business of his own. DaSilva had eaten and drunk his sake, and now he wanted some more entertainment. It was the work of a moment to climb out through the upper-floor window of his inn, teeter along a roof ridge, and jump to an alley. He had covered himself with a cloak, and in the dark he did not expect to be recognised. In any case, he was too drunk to care.

He was in an area of town dedicated apparently to inns and service establishments. There were lights ahead, and the sounds of music and laughter. He headed in that direction. A narrow alleyway seemed to offer a shortcut. He turned down it. Caution, and the experience of lawless streets in the cities of Europe, made him loosen his sword in its scabbard and look carefully in all directions. It was thus that he saw his vision.

To his right loomed a tall, dark building. A wooden fence hid all but the eaves of the structure. The eaves were illuminated by the faint light of lanterns between the houses and the fence. Presumably the lanterns were set in one of the tiny gardens the Japanners seemed to love. A small window opened high up under the eaves. A face peered out. DaSilva's heart leapt in his chest. It was the calm porcelain mask of his dreams, the one in the No plays that so fascinated him. He waited in the shadows. The mask leaned out of the window, and

200

he could see a slim arm, the delicate curve of a breast that presumably belonged to the mask. The mask bearer seemed to be beckoning to him, asking him to join her.

Sweat beaded his brow. He knew how deadly the Japanners were, how precarious was his own position. But his senses drove him on, aided and abetted by the wine he had drunk. Unthinkingly he leapt to the top of the wall. His sea boots were left in the alley behind him. The drink made him reckless and powerful. With a leap he had cleared the distance between the fence and the house. For a sailor used to clinging to swinging bars in all weathers, hanging from a house beam was no problem. There was a muffled shriek as the mask saw his looming figure. The mask disappeared as he swung himself quickly into the window.

He landed almost soundlessly in a dark room, his knees flexed. There was a sobbing breath beside him. He reached out a powerful hand. A soft shoulder and a quiet sob were what he had found. He explored further. The mask was there, and below it a smooth, soft body that trembled at his touch. His heavy hands slipped down the length of the figure. She was dressed in a simple cotton robe, and there was nothing beneath it but her trembling.

'Do not worry,' he said in his accented Japanese. 'You are very beautiful.' That about exhausted his conversational skills. Besides, it was time for action. He untied the sash that held the robe, wishing for a light to see the body and the mask. A sound attracted his attention. In a flash he realised that he had made a mistake. There was another person in the room. He wondered fleetingly, as his word slithered out of its scabbard, why they had not called for help. His blade touched the girl's neck.

'Who?' he demanded.

She whispered something breathlessly. There was a scratching of flint and steel, and the tiny glow of a candle in a paper lampion. Another masked girl, the mask a twin to the first, became visible. The figure with the lantern put a hand to her mouth at the sight of him. He held his sword threateningly near the first one's throat.

'Quiet!' he whispered. 'Quiet or I kill!'

The lust was rising in him as he saw the two girls in the dim light. They both wore the same thin cotton robes, and in the dim candlelight he could see their fresh young figures. Almost involuntarily his hand slipped from the girl's throat to her shoulder, then travelled to the swell of her throat. The mask expressed no emotion, but the body trembled at his touch. He did not want to ask what the masks were for, or know anything else but the feel of her flesh.

He turned to the other one and motioned her to kneel. She slid gracefully to her knees, her own mask hiding her face. He loosened the cotton robe on the girl before him and bared her upper body. Her breasts were small hillocks with dark, prominent nipples. He tweaked one experimentally. She did not move. The kneeling one muttered something under her breath, too quickly for him to catch the drift. He moved his sword warningly, and the one he held quieted. His hand went around the girl's waist to the tie of her sash, and the length of stiff fabric fell to the ground. The robe followed. He stepped back to admire the sight.

A slim body greeted his view. He wetted his forefinger in his mouth, then drew it down the length of the smooth body, from the rim of the mask, down the hollow of the throat. The breastbone distracted him, and he traced a line from nipple to nipple, then down the smooth swell of the belly to the moss underneath. His thick finger parted the smooth lips easily, and he felt a trace of moisture that was not his own. She shifted her weight and opened her legs slightly. The cavern was warm and moist, fitting his hard finger like a ring tailored for the use. His smile split his dark face. The mask seemed to growl at him, daring him to continue.

Remembering the other girl, he turned, afraid she was gone. She still sat there, the unreadable mask staring at him. He beckoned to her, and she came to him, seemingly unafraid.

He stood her by the other girl and loosened her clothes.

The two smooth, slim bodies were identical. He licked his lips expectantly. His dreams were being doubly gratified. He was usually not an imaginative man. Women were for the taking. He knew though that if he were discovered here, the owners of the house would kill him. He smiled again, half-drugged at the thought and the magic of the night. On this night, he would need something special.

He made them lie down on the rough mat. There was a ghost of a giggle as he bent them to the floor. Side by side, their nipples meshed and they looked like one body pressed against a mirror. Almost unordered they seemed to divine his wishes. Both raised their upper legs and thighs, exposing twin cunts to his view. The darker lips kissed to one another, the hairs meshing. He twisted their upper torsos so that the masks, both calm, both silent, faced him. His pantaloons were loosened in an instant. He knelt, each twin's lower leg between his

203

knees.

His first lunge was between the two bodies. Tough hairs scraped pleasingly against both sides of his rampant cock. He withdrew, and they pressed hungry mounds one against the other, squeezing him between them. He shoved forward again, the shaft trapped in the mossy vice, the tip of his member sliding slickly between two curving, muscular bellies.

He withdrew his cock again and, with a little effort, found the entrance to the left girl's hungry nether mouth. She seemed to tense for a second at the feel of his thick cock, but she only sighed when he gained entry to the narrow hole. He pressed forward, widening the smooth channel. A smooth, heavenly wetness covered his inflamed member. He pulled back, and the porcelainlike mask regarded him impassively, while brown arms hugged the other girl fiercely.

He pulled out and tried again. The right girl's mask shivered a bit as he forced his way into the lower mouth of its wearer. This time he rested for a while. He studied the masks. The differences between them must have meant something, but to him they were entirely opaque. The demands of his body called him back. He withdrew and thrust into the left girl again. Her body reacted furiously, clutching at her twin. He rammed into her now. The face reacted impassively, and the body trembled at his pushes but addressed itself to her twin. He withdrew and with an effort forced his way into the other.

Alternating between two channels, he worked himself to a climax. His hands were trembling from the effort. He felt his eyes starting from his head.

Still the calm faces stared back at him. The bodies moved with perfect measure, matching his moves, always transmitting their pleasure to one another, rarely acknowledging his presence directly.

The pressure built up in his balls until he thought he would burst. His movements became quicker and less controlled. As the flood of his juices welled up from his heavy balls, he was conscious enough to note that his cock was between their bodies again, roughly squeezed by their hairy mounds.

The spurts of his cream slathered their bellies, made them stick as they moved together. Only the tense quivering of their two bodies and the subdued moans served to tell him that the twins seemed to have reached their climaxes with him. As the last spurt left him he fell heavily on the two smooth, slight bodies beneath him. The combination of effort and drink hit him like a poleaxe, and he drifted off into darkness.

Rosamund smiled delightedly to herself in the dark. She loved the sense of adventure, and the slight touch of danger excited her so much that she rubbed her thighs together as she walked. Goemon, she decided, was going to have a difficult, if pleasant evening when they got back from his chore. Jiro, too, she decided generously. The entrance to the alley she sought was before her. Around her rose the shuttered houses of the rich townsmen of Miyako. Muffled sounds of music, an occasional bell, or the twitter of voices in the still night air reminded her that many of these imposing buildings were also places of business, some of which catered to night owls.

She opened her robe to expose more of her

breasts. They shone whitely in the light of a lantern set before a modest wooden door. She parted the lower folds too so that when she walked her legs would flash free. That would be enough, she decided, to attract the attention of any guard and give Goemon his chance. She slid into the alley, her heart pounding with excitement.

After his bath, Matsudaira Konosuke, governor of Miyako, known to certain intimates as Goemon, retired to a small enclosed room off his main bedroom. He unlocked a massive trunk and withdrew a long, silk-wrapped parcel. He unrolled the fabric and bowed reverently to the two swords it enclosed. Laying them aside, he began dressing himself.

He walked quickly through the deserted corridors of his mansion. Oko, Rosamund's maid, was kneeling at the entrance to her mistress's private room. She bowed at her master's approach. Her face, expressionless as usual, betrayed no surprise at his finery. He opened the sliding door. The room was empty. Goemon spun around.

'Where is she?' he demanded harshly.

Oko bowed. Face to the floor, she answered, 'Lady Rosamund went out.'

'Where to?'

'I do not know. She was dressed in her nun's habit.'

Goemon wasted no more time. Knowing his mistress, he feared the worst. He slipped out of the mansion by a side gate with a trick lock. Masking his face, he hurried through the streets, hoping to head Rosamund off. Notwithstanding his warning, he knew she had headed for the Sanjo Inn.

Chapter 13

Matsudaira Nobutaka, lord of Yoshida, sat in a small room reserved for his use and contemplated his actions. The room was secure, high up in the hidden roof of the Sanjo Inn. A ladder led up to it, and contrary to usual custom, all the walls were of hardened clay. There was no ceiling. He was guaranteed safe from observation and from eaves-dropping, and his bodyguard below ensured his privacy.

He reviewed his plans for the last time. The foreign captain had fulfilled his promise and delivered the guns. Mizuno-no-kami would arrive by midnight. His men would start drifting in soon after. Together they would proceed to the imperial palace. His own troops would have hold of the gates at his command. Strengthened by the guns now stored in Rokuro's godown near the palace, they would be more than a match for the city magistrate's troops and the imperial guard. The latter were only figuratively a guard. No shogun would trust them with any real duties.

They would enter the palace and tender their appeal to the Presence, who would immediately offer a rescript ordering them to dispose of the disobedient Tokugawa. With the Presence in their midst, they would split the Tokugawa forces, calling themselves loyalists and establishing a proper form of rule. His breath quickened at the thought. He studied the map of the town again, looking for flaws that he knew were not there. All he had to do now was wait for Mizuno-no-kami and for the right time. He put the plans away in his locked travelling chest.

He looked admiringly about him as he stretched luxuriously. The owners and builders of the Sanjo Inn had used a lot of thought to make their illustrious guests comfortable and a lot of ingenuity in making them safe. There were hidey holes everywhere for concealing guards. There were two secure rooms, the one in which he sat and another below. The inn was a maze, easy to defend, hard to attack. Though it looked like a three-storeyed structure, split levels, multiple stairways, and roofs that hid one another concealed two extra storeys. The clientele was exclusive, and the proprietor made sure he never entertained members of opposing factions.

Overall, the place was arranged and furnished in quiet excellence. The service was unobtrusive, almost invisible, and there were amenities here that even some country villas lacked. He thought again of the tiny Nō theatre, and at the memory of the earlier performance he licked scarred lips. His troupe was coming along, but just now, he felt like something fresh. Almost unbidden, his thoughts turned to the outside, to the refined city that spread out around him. Come midnight, it would be his own, but it would do no harm to precede that by a little bit.

He rose and wandered round the room. There was a post that overlooked the alley that ran beside the inn. Perhaps something new, something fresh would come along. He considered for a while, then made his way downstairs.

Matsudaira Nobutaka's patience was at an end. He had returned again and again to his lookout point, hiding his expectations even from himself. There had been nothing of any interest barring a couple of fat merchants and an itinerant doctor to pass through the alley. It was not a well-frequented passageway, but what had been a virtue was now a burden. His hands twitched, and his steps were jerky.

His samurai, who moved away from the observation post when the master was nearby, noted the familiar symptoms. He knew what they meant. Soon he or his comrades would have to go out and bring in another struggling figure. His master, he knew, was quite mad. But he was the master, lord of Yoshida, and loyalty to him was limitless. Mind you, thought the guard, there were compensations such as that young piece his master had brought in some weeks ago, who had eventually been enjoyed by all. He retreated into his thoughts again, as Yoshida peered out through the latticework into the alley again. He had ordered the lampions below lit, so that any potential attacker or victim would become instantly visible.

There was movement in the alley. A dark robe, A priest, Matsudaira thought. Then joy blazed up. No, a nun! And what a nun! he thought. Heavy breasts raised the black robe in front, and beautiful, well-formed legs flashed between the skirts every time she moved. Her head was covered by a kerchief, and her features were obscured, but he could not miss the chance. He muttered rapid orders, and two of his men left the room in a hurry.

Once she felt the bag over her head, Rosamund stopped struggling. Her hands ripped open the package in her sleeves, and fine white rice powder sifted down as she was carried through what seemed like endless halls.

At last she was deposited unceremoniously on a tatami mat. A male voice, the first she had heard since her kidnapping, ordered someone to leave. A sash was thrown around her arms, pinioning them to her sides, and the sack was removed from her head.

She was in a small but richly appointed room. Several lamps lit the interior, which was of polished wood. The wall panels were painted with peonies and the ceiling with butterflies. A man was staring down at her. His face was brooding, with a hint of cruelty and madness peering out from his dark eyes. His once handsome face was disfigured by two scars that crossed from each cheekbone to the opposite side of the chin.

He dropped suddenly on her legs and tore them apart. She struggled, but he was stronger and more experienced. He knelt there, and his head snaked forward in a pecking motion. His mouth closed over the soft flesh of her inner thigh, and he bit in ecstasy.

She screamed with the pain, and he licked roughly at the marks of his teeth, then burrowed farther up into the soft, fleshy part of her crotch. The wonderful smell of her womanhood attracted him, and he roughly licked and sucked at her full lips. His mouth found her prominent clitoris, and he sucked it in and chewed at it hungrily.

Rosamund screamed again, more in hopes of rescue than in shock or pain. The rough treatment her cunt was receiving was starting to get to her. He changed his tactics as her insides started getting wet. A long and incredibly mobile tongue searched the length of her slit then probed the length of her wet channel. His oral digit seemed to touch and search every corner of her hungry nether mouth. Her heels drummed on his back, which only increased the tempo of his tongue's manoeuvres. He raked a hand along the length of her flank, and she gasped with unexpected pleasure. He bit at the lips of her cunt again, and she responded with a gasp and a push of her loins into his jaws. His eyes closed, he savoured the delicious smell and taste of her luxurious cunt.

Squeezing and pinching the mound of her buttocks, his hand edged between the hills of her ass. His long finger invaded her clenched anus and probed at the muscular ring. For a moment it objected to the penetration; then she relaxed and his probing finger slipped easily inside her. It was followed by a second finger as the other hand invaded her cunt in a similar fashion. Licking and biting her alternately, he worked his fingers into her together from both entrances.

Delighted by the pain and the attention of his fingers and tongue, Rosamund started to lose control. Her hips swivelled in an anguished attempt to swallow more of him. Her thighs clenched about his ears and knocked his topknot askew. She kicked her heels against his back as powerfully as she could, driving him on in greater frenzy to penetrate her. He withdrew his face to contemplate her form just as the first spasm of her orgasm hit her.

Bouncing forward, she tried to force more and more of his fingers into her eagerly opened orifices. He watched with delight as she came over his fingers, spreading her juices over his hands and the matting underneath her. Then the unusual appearance of her pussy came into his conscious attention. On her inner thigh was tattooed a red rose in full bloom. It grew out from between the full lips of her cunt, out from a thicket of the palest soft blonde hair he had seen.

He reared back in surprise as her moaning climax ended. He threw himself forward and tore off her robe. Full, pink-tipped breasts stared back at him on a white body of full, rounded curves. He pulled off her swathing hood, and the full glory of her incredible golden hair tumbled to the mat.

'A foreigner! A southern barbarian woman!' he exclaimed in surprise. The look on his face grew fixed, and his entire frame seemed to shudder. 'I have never had one such! How wonderful!' He squatted back on his haunches to contemplate her beautiful form, but the reality was too much for him. With a cry he launched himself forward. His strong hands clutched greedily at her full breasts, crushing the mounds and bruising the fair skin. His hard prick unerringly found her sopping hole, and he rammed himself inside, up to the hilt. His hairs meshed with hers, and he rocked forward as if in his dying throes.

Rosamund gasped at the onslaught and the sudden weight, but the familiar feel of a male body upon her brought her to her senses. He would have to be killed definitely now, she thought, but in the meantime...

He thrust at her with all the power in his loins. His mouth covered hers, and his tongue snaked inside, tasting her delightful mouth. She could detect the smell and taste of her own lower mouth on his breath as she sucked his probing, agile tongue into her mouth. He rocked into her furiously, and she rose towards her second climax. She clenched her legs against him and drove her heels into his sides. The pain in her bound arms stimulated her passion, and she felt she was exploding.

Suddenly his probing at her cunt stopped. She tried to urge him on, knowing he had not finished and knowing too that she could come a third time. He slapped her breasts viciously, which only brought a smile of satisfaction to her lips; then he pushed himself away, tearing at her locked legs. His eyes were fixed on her face. He pulled her to a sitting position with rough movements, then pushed her mouth down on his erect prick. Her long blonde hair fell over her face, and he clutched a handful, obscuring her face. He fucked determinedly into her mouth.

She gagged at first at the rapid and painful movements, but they were no worse than what she had forced Goemon to do to her, and this prick was certainly no larger than Jiro's. Her mouth and throat adjusted. She could taste her own juices at first, but soon that was overwhelmed by the male flavour of her attacker. His cock trip-hammered into her

213

mouth, and she rounded the orifice to make it pleasanter for him. When she could, she gave a quick lick to the tip of his erection, which would make his whole frame quiver. Little drops of clear liquid appeared at the tip, and she tasted those with appreciation. Every once in a while she would scrape his shaft with her teeth, reminding him silently to have more respect for the source of his delights. At each sharp touch he would twist or slap her hanging tits painfully. In the dark, hidden by her tresses, she could barely see the approach and retreat of his muscular belly.

Suddenly he stiffened. The veins in the underside of his shaft began to pulse. A dribble of milky fluid appeared at the tip. She prepared herself to swallow the flood to come. Instead, he withdrew himself roughly from her mouth. He pushed her forward so that her head was to the floor, and her full ass rose enticingly in the air.

He stood behind her. From that position the view was almost irresistible. The tattooed flower was only partly visible, but its stem rose, with one leaf reaching coyly forward to the clit and another pouting the way to the clenched, starfish-like anus. The perfect white hemispheres of her ass were divided by a long white line that rose from the lips of the cunt and disappeared in the swell of the back of the hips, merging gracefully with her spine. The length of the vertical line was pleasantly hairless. It glistened with the juices that had run out of her pleasured body.

Matsudaira's cock was bubbling, almost in agony of frustration. He aimed at the tiny target and with one swift strike penetrated her rear entrance. The broad cockhead met rubbery resistance at first, but then the muscles parted and he found himself deep in her, her entire form lying defeated before him. Slowly he reached for her dangling tits and massaged each in turn. He gradually increased the pressure of his fingers, driving the sensitive nipples into the milk-white flesh as the movement of his lions against her buns quickened.

A growl came from his mouth as his eyes seemed to start out of his head. Rosamund felt him grunting as the painful pleasure spear rammed into her. She undulated against his muscular frame, the pleasure she was expecting rising from her toes to the top of her head. As she started twitching in expectation, his own climax hit. He ground the sandpaper of his hairs against her ass. His hands locked like vices into her breasts, compressing them against her ribcage. As spurt after spurt of thick, milky fluid inundated her insides, he clung to her unmoving, teeth clenched into the skin of her shoulder. She came too, just as the last of his spasms spurted out of his balls. She arched against him, pushing him back with brute force, as if trying to become one with her violater.

At last he pulled himself from her and sat back contemplating her. The fixed stare returned to his eyes. She lay there in her naked glory on the floor, waiting for the next act.

'A foreign whore, eh? Disguised as a nun!' The tone of his voice altered. 'A spy! Aren't you a foreign spy?' He slapped her face. 'Admit it! You're a spy, coming to uncover my plans.' His brows lashed into her face as his voice rose almost to a shriek. 'I'll have you some more, then turn you over to my men for questioning . . .'

She licked her lips nervously. She had only

intended a reconnaissance, not a full penetration. Goemon would be furious. *And I*, she thought along more practical lines, *will probably be dead*. Action suited thought. He was exhausted by his efforts, she could see. Her foot lashed out suddenly in a blow to the heart that would kill him. Okiku had taught her well.

But Matsudaira had not been known as a formidable fighter for nothing. His body slipped aside with ease. He caught her leg as it whistled by. Her second kick, a full roundhouse, grazed the top of his head, dazing him for a moment. She rolled to her feet and, since there was no retreat, advanced for the kill. Pride, or perhaps muzziness induced by the kick, stopped him from calling for help. She leapt at him and kicked, but his trained reflexes took over. Still kneeling, he shifted one knee to the rear and pivoted. His left hand, farther from Rosamund, swept one foot out from under her and rose higher than his head. His right hand pushed roughly into her soft belly and pushed her to the ground. She fell, and her head smacked the tatami with a crack.

She came to with a feeling of great discomfort and with Matsudaira's scarred face leering into her own. She was on her back, but only the upper portion was being supported. Her legs were tied high in the air, her hips at the level of his as he stood. Her hands were still tied behind her, and her legs were spread. Her heavy breasts fell down over her chin. She felt as if she were looking at his face over a rampart.

He tittered as he admired her full cunt and the flower it bore. Seeing she was awake, he looked at her face.

'One more time. I'll have you like this; then we can ask some questions.' He grinned unpleasantly. 'I have some excellent ways of asking questions, spy. Unfortunately, you'll be no good for anyone after them, so we'll have to dispose of you ...' His voice trailed off as he advanced on her.

The tip of his prick stroked up and down the length of her exposed vulva. He played with both of them, covering the shaft with the fat lips of her cunt, smacking the **V** of her thighs with his pole, teasing the prominent clitoris. Unwillingly, she began to respond. At length the game grew too exciting for him. He arched her body with a hand and bent his knees. At the angle his cock was in she felt excessively tight, and he enjoyed the slow slide into her well-lubricated twat.

Rosamund had one weapon left, one she had practised at length. She felt the length of his shaft penetrating her, banging against the front wall of her belly. The heavy, hairy bag knocked against her ass, and she smiled at him sweetly, then clenched her vaginal muscles. The grip was so powerful that he screamed in surprise and pain. He tried to pull out, but his shaft was caught in a muscular vice. His hands pounded on her thighs, but the reaction was one of absolute pain and terror. He screamed tinnily, like a rat caught in a trap. Automatically his hand dropped to his waist, to the powerful muscles that held him and pained him at his most sensitive member. The back of his hand brushed against a hard object. Reflexes took over, and the tanto dagger was in his hand before the thought. He raised it high to bring it down on the terrifying demon beneath him who was slowly strangling his life away.

Chapter 14

Goemon, dressed in his finery, finally reached the alley that led to the Sanjo Inn's main entrance. He drew a deep breath in relief. There were no unusual sounds emanating from the inn. It appeared peaceful and restful in the night. Goemon was thankful that Miyako citizens were a quiet and sober lot, even in the rich districts such as this. He hoped he had arrived before Rosamund. For a while he waited; then impatience got the better of him and he stepped into the alley. A low-pitched whistle stopped him. In the darkness he could make out the bulk of a familiar figure, motioning to him from another alleyway.

'You're early,' whispered Jiro.

'What are *you* doing here?'

'I followed the captain here. He climbed into a window of the inn.'

'What?' whispered Goemon.

'I'm as surprised as you are. He was walking down

the alley, and I was about to finish him off, when he gave a sudden leap, and the next thing I saw, he was climbing into a window above. He's as agile as a monkey, notwithstanding his fat.'

Goemon could not help but smile in the dark. The captain was no fatter than Jiro, but the latter was used to being the largest person around, and the captain's size seemed to arouse some hidden antagonism.

'It seems our plan is getting complicated. Though if he's part of the plot, why climb through the window?'

'He was pretty drunk at the time,' grinned Jiro in the dark.

'That might explain it. Then of course, he's also a foreigner and unpredictable. Where is Okiku? She said she'd finished the affair quickly.'

As Goemon spoke, Jiro's attention focused elsewhere. He thought he heard stealthy sounds down the alley that led to the main entrance.

'And to add to all our troubles,' Goemon continued, unaware of his friend's tension, 'Rosamund has gone off on her own. I imagine she thinks she is helping someone or doing some act of bravery. At least she has not arrived here –'

The sounds repeated themselves, and Jiro hushed Goemon with a movement of his hand. There was a distinct clink of metal from within the alleyway Goemon had been about to enter.

Silently both men ran to the alley and headed down it. They reached the entrance to the inn. It was closed as before, a blank face presented to the world. They were standing before it, wondering what to do, when the door clicked open.

Okiku, in her brown clothes, stood before them.

Her blade was bloody.

Okiku had found Mizuno a hard man to follow. He was cautious, turning to check at each intersection, scanning the roof ridges, stopping for long moments in shadowy entrances to houses and mansions. The dark was her ally, but he, too, appeared familiar with it. Her problem was solved as soon as she realised where he was headed – the Sanjo Inn. Now she hurried ahead of him, checking back to see that he followed. It took them a long time to reach the inn from the kuge quarter. She hid in the entrance to a merchant's house as he checked carefully around him before entering the alley that housed the main entrance to the inn.

He ducked inside hurriedly, knowing he was not followed. As he passed a shadowy entrance, he felt the rise of a breeze. Okiku's blade passed harmlessly over his head, neatly shearing off his black gauze hat and his erect old-fashioned topknot. He spun around, his mouth spitting the tiny needles that he had kept there the whole time. The tiny missiles distracted his assassin so that he could draw his antique blade. It flashed in the pale glow of the lantern that marked the entrance to the Sanjo Inn.

As she struck, Okiku knew the blow would miss. It would have been so easy, a twin-handed horizontal strike from the back that would have neatly decapitated him. But she was used to practising with a much taller man, Jiro, and the high hat gave the illusion of height.

Expecting the needles, she ducked them easily and recovered from the swing in time to parry his blow. His scabbard, hanging by cords from his sash, hampered his movements somewhat. She stabbed at his belly underhand and, as he parried, returned some of his own medicine. Her left hand flashed forward, and a cloud of powder blew into the kuge's face. It blinded him for a moment, time enough for her to kick at his belly.

He ducked the powder, but she felt her foot hit something that gave. He grunted and rolled with the blow, lying almost winded on the floor of the alley, back against the inn's entrance. She brought her sword down two handed, at his head. He blocked with his curved blade, twisting her straight one momentarily into a bind. She recovered and leapt high to avoid his countering horizontal cut. As she leapt he fumbled with his hand. A panel in the door swung open, and he tumbled through. The panel shut with a click.

Okiku landed in a crouch, then without pause leapt again as high as she could. She again landed in a crouch on top of the brick wall that circled the inn. Below her Mizuno was pointing to the door in agitation, facing two rough-looking samurai with Matsudaira crests on their robes. She held her straight sword before her and leapt. The blade pierced one guard's shoulder, emerging below his kidney. By the time her full weight had hit him, he was dead. Using the corpse as a fulcrum, Okiku cartwheeled backwards like an enormous rubber doll. The heel of one foot struck the other guard full in the chin. She caught her balance, and her cupped hand came around at his temple and ear. There was an unpleasant cracking sound, and the second guard fell. She groped for her sword as Mizuno disappeared into the inn. Outside she could hear what sounded like familiar steps. Taking a risk, she opened the inn's massive front door. Goemon and Jiro stood without.

'Hurry! Mizuno just ran in. I'm after him.' She left in a silent padding run, her freed blade in her hand.

The entrance hall of the inn was dark. A figure loomed before her. A waiting guard. She wondered how Mizuno had got in ahead of her and where he had gone. A tiny dirk slipped into her hand, and without pausing she threw it left-handed. It took the man in the throat.

She touched the narrow stairway before her. It vibrated. Mizuno was going up, and she hurriedly followed. She felt no movement at the top of the stairs but rolled through nontheless. Since she was rolling, her feet did not trip the cord stretched across the top of the stairs. Mizuno was hurrying ahead of her, staggering somehow and breathing noisily.

She hurried after him, her trained feet making no sound. He turned and saw her. She saw his sleeve flap and spun to the side. A looped cord whipped by her and fell on the floor. She threw a small bag of powder at him. Mizuno ducked around a corner. The bag burst on a pillar, staining it black. A tiny bonsai on the table at the end of the corridor started to wilt in the dark. The corridor she was on ended in a T. She followed Mizuno down one arm, and he ducked through a sliding shoji into a room beyond. The room he was in was empty, but beyond the shoji at the far end there was a pale light and the sound of frenzied movement.

When DaSilva awoke he was alone in the dark. He could not tell how long he had been unconscious. He groped heavily for his sword. The hilt clanked against the rings on his hands. He rose and adjusted his pantaloon hurriedly. The girls were nowhere to be seen. He could see the slightly greyer square of

the window. Two sounds distracted him. From far
below he could hear movement and what seemed
like a muffled cry.

He crouched by the window and looked out.
There seemed to be movement down below. A flash
of motion caught his eye. The way back was blocked.
He licked his lips nervously. Another way might
exist, but it seemed the household was about to
wake. A sliding door opened before him. He
crouched by the window. In the dark he could hear
someone moving. The figure resolved itself into a
cotton robe and a pale porcelain mask. Relieved, he
rose and familiarly slid a hand into the robe,
squeezing gently at a soft breast. There was a quick
intake of breath and the beginning of a cry, which he
managed to stifle with his hand. He felt the breast
again. The shape was different, plumper and flatter
on the chest. The same mask but a different girl –
and she was ready to scream.

Chapter 15

Satsuki straightened her torso. Obligingly, Rokuro stopped his pumping. His thick cock lay quiescent in her while his hands pinched her erect nipples. He nibbled gently at her ear while she arranged herself on his lap, careful not to disturb the wonderful instrument in her. He was her first client, and she wanted his time with her, short as it was to be, to be perfect. She reached carefully for the biwa and began playing softly. Her body swayed to the rhythm of the music, rubbing her inside tissues against his tumescence. He smiled in delight and closed his eyes. She switched to a more rollicking tune, a country ballad, and the speed of her motions increased.

Finally she started playing the music of the Awa dance. His hands beat the cadence on her thighs, her back, her buttocks, while her ass rose and bounced on his prick in ever-increasing tempo. He *oofed* every time she came down.

Now the tempo raced. She closed her eyes to slits in pleasure and added a sideways shake to her dancing, just as the dancers did when aroused. She felt her nipples expanding, and her cunt opened, wanting to swallow more and more of the delicious throbbing length that ran up her almost to the full.

At last they cried out together as the biwa sounded a triumphant chord. He grasped her hips and shook her as a dog would shake a rag. She forced herself down on him, grinding every drop of come out of his spouting tube, pushing him down into the springy tatami floor until marks rose on the skin of his shins and knees. Spurt after spurt inundated her insides, and she felt herself melting onto his lap.

She fell forward, and he let her go. His softening prick slid out of her hole with a barely perceptible plop. Their liquids ran down both their thighs. He was panting but still smiled sadly. He would have to leave her now, for a short while, at least. In time, he thought, he might come again – as a victor and lord, not a mere merchant. The pleasure of anticipation was almost as good as the pleasure he had got from the now shrunken prick that lolled exhausted and sopping on his thigh.

She turned on her side, then on her back, her legs to either side of him. He could see the length of her warm slit. It oozed moisture, a combination of them both. The bushy mound was dripping, like a moss forest after the dew. Her dark nipples were flat with satiation, as her eyes half-closed in satisfaction.

'I must go,' he mouthed.

Her hands fell to her sides, still holding the lute and the plectrum. 'On me, once more. To feel again.'

He grinned in triumph. To have a professional women beholden to him would tickle any man's pride. He lunged forward and smacked his torso hard onto her, burying his mouth to her neck. The axhead-shaped plectrum of hard wood came up and drove deep into the back of his neck, severing the spinal cord. He was dead.

Captain Agostinho DaSilva released the warm, soft breast and removed his gaze from the mask. His drunkenness seemed to drop from him like a cloak as he saw Jiro's menacing figure before him. He breathed audibly through his mouth, then smiled. White teeth flashed from a coal-black beard and mahogany face. A diamond stud in his ear winked in the lamplight.

'Guard, no?' he inquired softly in poor Japanese.

'I'll kill you myself,' the man facing him replied in English.

'An Englander, are you? I had an Englander prisoner once. Paid good ransom too. But you look like a Japanese.' His English was precise and unnatural, but Jiro understood him well. The captain slid back and drew his long rapier. His leather sheath swung at his side.

The captain bowed, his left foot extended. 'Don Agostinho DaSilva at your service, senhor.'

Jiro, his hands at his sides, his weight distributed equally on both legs, bowed in return. 'Miura Jiro of Miyako.' He took a step backwards and drew his two-handed katana. His lacquered wooden sheath hung behind from his sash.

The two men took a few seconds to take one another's measure. Both were big men, the captain perhaps a trifle heavier, Jiro's shoulders a trifle wider. Large hands held their weapons easily. The captian's rapier pointed straight ahead in a high guard in quarte. Jiro stood in chudan kamae, sword forward, weight balanced between both feet.

Without a preparatory sign of any kind, DaSilva lunged. His rapier hissed by Jiro's chest as the samurai turned and deflected the blade with the concave back of his own. The steel lengths whined off one another, sounding like giant mosquitoes. Before Jiro could riposte, the captain had recovered from his lunge and was standing in guard again. He grinned, and Jiro ruefully twitched the muscles of his chest and felt the thin flow of blood down the inside of his robe.

The captain smiled heartily. He leapt forward, feinting a lunge and then striking with a backhand blow under Jiro's guard. Jiro swept the straight blade to his right, then struck with the long pommel of his curved katana at DaSilva's wrist. At the same time he seized the wrist and swept the captain's feet from under him with his left foot. The captain fell to the floor. Jiro advanced one step and stabbed down with his blade. Only a wild stop thrust from the captain sprawled on the tatami checked Jiro's rush and allowed the captain to twist his feet. They struck at one another's heads. The swords screeched together until the round, flat guard of the katana and the bell of the rapier clicked together.

Jiro's two-handed grip would have been decisive here, corps-a-corps, but DaSilva seized Jiro's wrist. They wrestled together. Brute strength was at work. Facing one another, each holding the other's wrist, they could have been a pair of entranced lovers but for the bright blades. Each increased the pressure of his hand, which was reflected in the rictuses on both men's faces. They manoeuvred for position, only their feet in motion.

The captain stood with his back to a paper-glazed shoji. Hs face contorted with effort. There was a sudden movement and sound as the shoji was roughly shaken by a heavy object. For a moment his concentration was shaken. Jiro leaned deeply to his right. He loosened DaSilva's wrist, and the palm of his hand slid past the other man's armpit while he twisted his own body to the right, raising his left hand high.

The captain flipped over, landing heavily on his left shoulder. Without pause Jiro drew his short sword from its scabbard at his sash and ripped the captain's belly from solar plexus to groin. The captain gurgled, and his grip on Jiro's right wrist relaxed. Jiro twisted loose, dropped his small sword, and knelt by the supine captain. He supported the long blade with his left palm and with his right drove the curved blade deep into the captain's heart. He retrieved his weapons as from the fosuma door behind him came a woman's furious scream and a man's roar. In two giant strides he smashed through the sliding doors into the room beyond.

Okiku launched herself desperately at Mizuno. The neighbouring room sounded occupied, and any moment now he might recover his voice or make a sound that would bring him help. She swept his feet out from under him. He fell on her, and the sounds of his fall were muffled. His hands sought her throat. She tried to roll over, then struck with cupped hands at his face. He reared back, then slammed his forehead into her face. Only a quick turn of her face saved her from a smashed nose. As it was, she was almost stunned, clinging to him with the remains of her strength.

Automatically she sought the best hold, trying to pin him to her. He struggled in the dark. Under her loose clothes he noticed her soft curves for the first time. His hands were locked behind her, and hers were clawing at his back. Moving his chest he explored the softness of her breasts. Yes, she was a woman. Surprise held him for a mere moment; then with a wriggle she managed to throw him off. Faint sounds of combat from an adjoining room made Okiku renew her struggle. She had to finish him before the guards arrived.

She broke free, and the two antagonists slowly climbed to their feet. He was weaving drunkenly, and she felt little better. Harsh sounds came from his throat, but still he did not call out. In the pale light it became apparent that her kick in the alley had damaged his throat. He was unable to make a sound. She stood with her back to a darkened shoji. To her left slight illumination from an adjacent room illuminated the scene. Suddenly he charged at her, hands chopping accurately at her neck and crotch. The second blow caught her, and she fell backwards, against the shoji. The shoji did not give. A heavy body supported her from the other side of the fragile paper barrier for the second she needed.

She twisted aside. Mizuno snarled breathlessly in triumph and reached for her again. She stepped into his embrace. The two kozuka she had taken from her sleeve slid slickly under his ribs. They met at his heart, and he fell, his look of triumph turning to one of surprise.

Okiku spun around, ready to attack whoever was behind her, when a scream of fear and pain reached her ears from the lighted room at her side. She slid the shoji open onto a large hall, half of which was occupied by a covered stage.

On the stage lay a familiar blonde figure. She was naked. Her legs were held apart in the air by two cords tied to the beams over the stage. Her hair lay like a pillow, supporting her shoulders. A stringy man stood between her legs, bridging the distance between them by a fleshy branch that penetrated deep into the blonde's flesh at the juncture of her legs. His mouth was open in a scream, and the naked blade in his hand was blurring towards Rosamund's helpless body. Okiku threw her remaining shaken.

His eyes staring madly at his captive, Matsudaira Nobutaka poised his short sword before bringing it down on her spread body. There was a buzzing sound. A bright metallic star knocked his tanto blade away. A second cut raggedly into his wrist, forcing him to drop the dagger. With an effort he tore himself away from his captive's grip on him. The blonde woman yowled in anger and frustration and spat curses at him in a mixture of bad Japanese, English, and Spanish. He leapt back, and the sliding wall to his left burst apart. A giant samurai stood there, sword poised, his shoulders covered with tatters from the fusuma, his chest bloody.

Matsudaira spun around and rushed for the stage exit. He ran onto the bridge and stopped. A figure stood there blocking his way. Matsudaira's nerve broke for a second.

'Who – are you? Wh-what is this?' he stammered.

'Lights!' commanded the figure before him. Behind Matsudaira someone quickly uncovered the lampions. Before him Lord Matsudaira of Yoshida saw the figure of a samurai. He was a short man, rather stocky. His topknot was newly oiled and lay across his shaved pate like a line of stiff ink. He was dressed in an expensive white silk robe dyed with a blue wave. His sash was a stiff gold brocade. In it were stuck two fine swords. Their cord hafts were pure white picked out with gold ornaments. The rounded sword guards were enamelled in gold, and the sheaths were white as well. All the finery did nothing to hide the severity of the face. The samurai regarded Matsudaira with an unwavering gaze.

'Who are you? What do you want?' demanded Matsudaira with more strength.

'Lord Matsudaira Nobutaka of Yoshida, you who plotted against the shogun's government, you are about to die.'

Matsudaira gasped, more in surprise than in fear. 'Who are you who speak through the night making accusations?'

In a deep voice the man opposite him answered, 'I go by the name Goemon, but my name is Matsudaira Konosuke, and my title is governor of Miyako. My authority is *this*!' and he drew his great sword in its scabbard, turning it so that the flat of the guard would show.

On it, picked out in gold on the black steel, were three hollyhock leaves in a circle – the personal mark of the shogun.

Matsudaira's eyes opened, but before he could formulate a response, a second voice came from behind him.

'Matsudaira Nobutaka. For killing the prioress of Dosojin-ji temple and violating its inhabitants, you shall die, as your men have before you.'

Matsudaira spun around. Behind him the giant samurai advanced onto the No stage, sword in hand.

A third voice joined the other two, high and feminine this time. 'Matsudaira Nobutaka. For kidnapping and raping my friend, a foreign lady, you shall die.' Lord Matsudaira searched the hidden eyes of the figure before him. It was that of the ninja spy, muffled in dark brown garments, straight sword held at the ready. He fell back a step. The ninja slashed twice, and Rosamund's legs fell to the ground. She breathed heavily, and the tableau held for a second; then, gathering her strength, she searched her scattered clothes and rose tottering to her feet. With an inarticulate scream she rushed at Matsudaira and swung a glittering weighted chain at his head.

His trained warrior reflexes took over. He ducked and then ran sideways, leaping over the low barrier that bounded the walkway from the stage.

Before he could cry out, he felt rather than saw Goemon's blade come at him. He turned and ran back to the stage. Rosamund swung wildly at him again. He saw his short sword on the boards of the stage and without pause scooped it up and stabbed upward at the ninja who was blocking his way.

Okiku blocked the thrust with the side of her blade. Her foot lashed out in a roundhouse kick, taking Matsudaira on the chin. He spun away, then stiffened in pain. Jiro withdrew his sword from the daimyo's side, his face a glazed mask.

Matsudaira raised his hand and took two paces back to the centre of the stage. Before him he saw Rosamund's naked figure, her golden hair blazing. He raised his hand and brought it down at the shining beauty of it. This time she was more accurate. The weight on the end of her manryukusari flicked out and hit his fist, crushing the fingers and sending the blade spinning into the dark corners of the hall. He stood there for a second, trying to speak, trying to call the guards, trying to remember how he had got to that place at that time. He never noticed Goemon's sharp blade, pointed in the air, which came with a rush at his neck.

A heavy round object hit the boards of the stage and bounced once. Matsudaira's torso followed, staining the floor like Chinese lacquer.

With his left hand Matsudaira Konosuke, governor of Miyako, personal agent of the shogun and distant kinsman of the corpse, withdrew a handful of clean white paper from the bosom of his robe and wiped the length of his blade. It winked again in the candlelight.

The four agents turned silently to go. Bloodstained paper fluttered onto the headless corpse as the lights went out on the stage.

The four sat in the inner confines of the governor's mansion. The small room, plainly furnished, overlooked a small garden and three blank whiteplastered walls. The sliding shoji were open to let in any passing breeze. Four trays on little legs were arranged in an open triangle, one at the head and right, two at the left. The open side of the square allowed them all a view of the garden, lit faintly by a single stone lantern.

They were formally dressed. Goemon, his back to the tokonoma alcove, wore a short black coat with his family's crest on sleeves and back. Jiro was similarly attired, though unlike his smaller friend, his pate was unshaven. Rosamund and Okiku sat facing him, each in a fine silk kimono tied with a broad sash. Outside the door, a faithful Oko awaited their needs and guarded their privacy.

Goemon raised his cup. 'To us. We have done, I

233

believe, quite well. Bottoms up.'

They raised their cups, echoing, 'Bottoms up.'

From beyond the shoji, which was not opened completely, came a strange voice: 'I second that.'

Jiro swivelled to one foot, his short sword in his hand. Rosamund spun around, and her loaded chain buzzed rapidly from her sleeve. Only Okiku and Goemon remained unmoved.

'You are getting careless in your old age, Hanzo,' said Okiku calmly as she drained her cup. 'I heard you land from the roof.'

'Please enter and join us in a drink, Master Hanzo.'

A shadow appeared on the shoji as Hattori Hanzo, the shogun's spymaster, moved into the light. He chuckled softly.

'No, thank you, Lord Matsudaira. I understand you identified the problem?'

'And solved it,' added Goemon.

'The Presence will be most pleased. Were there any complications? Loose ends...?'

'None. It is finished.'

'Very well. I will go. Perhaps we may meet again. There is no need for you to trouble yourself. I will carry the news to Edo.' There was a faint sound from the eaves of the mansion, and the shadow was gone.

After they had eaten and the sake bottles had added up, Goemon grinned at his friends.

'Actually I lied to Hanzo. There are two loose ends, I think.'

Jiro raised an eyebrow. 'What? We cleaned them all out. I don't think there was anyone we forgot. In any case, with the guns confiscated and destroyed, and the heads of the plot all dead, we can let bygones be bygones.'

'Not quite,' said Goemon as he moved his legged tray aside deliberately and leaned to his left. 'No, not quite. We have a smaller matter of insubordination.' At the last word his hand flashed out and grabbed Rosamund's collar, pulling her face down to the floor and spilling her drink. He pulled her robe down her shoulders to pinion her thrashing arms. She squealed in surprise and apprehension.

'Yes, insubordination. You could have been killed, you hellion! I wouldn't have found Matsudaira but for your screams, true, but I wouldn't have had to look so far but for your attempt at playing the spy.'

She struggled to loose herself, but Goemon's hand kept her down. 'Okiku, help me!' the blonde called.

Okiku leaned over and, smiling, pulled Rosamund's skirts up, exposing her long perfect legs and ass. 'Not me, my love. I had palpitations when I saw you tied there, and I think we really should punish you.' She smacked the blonde's bum once, very loudly. A pink flush marred the perfect white half spheres.

Rosamund twisted her neck around. 'Jiro, you're on my side. Didn't I do right?'

Jiro rose to his full height leisurely. 'No, Rosamund. You were almost lost to us. That is a cardinal sin. I'm afraid you must bear the consequences.' He slipped off his robe and stood before her naked. His massive member, half-erect, jutted straight forward like the muzzle of a gun.

Goemon laughed. 'Not so quick. We must teach her first.' He straddled her head, clamping it between his knees while divesting himself of his clothing. His cock was an erect tower, his jewel bag resting on the warm nest of her soft hair. Beneath

235

him she tried to bite the inside of his thighs, but was frustrated by his strong grip.

Okiku laughed and leaned forward. Her full lips engulfed Goemon's swollen member. She sucked loudly, and it slid tantalisingly into the depths of her cheeks. She reached out and took Jiro's cock in her hand. Jerking the loose skin back and forth, she made the pole harden and thicken to the quality she desired. With her other hand she tickled him under his swinging bag.

Jiro knelt beside Rosamund and with Goemon's help rapidly divested her of her clothing. Then, while one held Rosamund down the other administered measured smacks to her flushing behind, they undressed in turn before her.

Rosamund was breathing heavily by the time her three lovers were ready for her. The two men, under Okiku's directions, lay on Rosamund's either side. Goemon, behind her, pinched the flesh of her buttocks viciously. Tiny goosebumps appeared, and she twitched at each pinch, while still struggling to extricate herself.

Jiro, before her, measured out the same medicine to her full breasts. Okiku squatted before the three of them on the floor, showing off her perfect delicate cunt, which she teased with her fingers. The opening was clearly visible to Rosamund, who licked her lips hungrily at the sight.

'Goemon,' asked Okiku, 'is there anything you wish to say?'

'Yes.' Then, emphasising each word with a pinch that made Rosamund squirm, he said in a measured tone, 'You must... never... scare... us... by... putting... yourself... at... risk... in... that... way!'

'But we won!' she yowled through tears and the beginning of a smile. The smile deepened as Goemon moved his hips forward and slid himself home into her well-lubricated ass. As soon as he had finished and could rest comfortably, Jiro moved forward. He raised her upper thigh and poised for a moment, then his own massive, stiff prick forced itself into her smooth, slick cunt. The three rested for a moment without a motion, enjoying the soaking of the men's members.

Okiku rose and walked to the joined end and squatted again. She ran her hand over the joint of the three bodies, and all three twitched. The tangle of legs met in a colourful swirl of black and gold, the men's bags hiding the woman's flesh entrances. The bright red of the rose tattoo shone like a jewel. Okiku admired the sight for a short while, then rose and cradled Rosamund's face in her crotch. Rosamund kissed the moist forest, and her tongue darted out hungrily.

Okiku sighed with pleasure and said, 'Let us begin,' as the men reached for her.